Badawi

Badawi

Mohed Altrad

Translated from the French by
Adriana Hunter

Black Cat
New York

Badawi was first published in France by Actes Sud.

First English-language edition published by Grove Atlantic, September 2016

Published simultaneously in Canada
Printed in the United States of America

ISBN 978-0-8021-2579-8
eISBN 978-0-8021-9016-1

Black Cat
an imprint of Grove Atlantic
154 West 14th Street
New York, NY 10011

Distributed by Publishers Group West

groveatlantic.com

16 17 18 19   10 9 8 7 6 5 4 3 2 1

I started to seek a state of rest in compiling this book, and have made it a lament for home and for loved ones. It serves no purpose and will be of no help, but I have done everything my strength would allow.

—Usâma Ibn Munqidh (1172),
The Book of Camps and Homes

Badawi

1

The child waited till the woman lifted aside the blanket at the entrance to the tent and slipped outside. Then he got up quietly, pulled a length of cloth around his shoulders, and went out himself. There was no edge along the top of the hills. The occasional animal cry breaking the darkness seemed to trace their outline for a fleeting moment. But the velvet of the desert and the sky swiftly cleaved together again, as if the land were succumbing to the moon's caress.

The child watched the woman's dark shape hurrying through the night. From time to time a star stole a muted spark from the little coins edging the gossamer fabric along her forehead, or picked out the sheen on the bleached chicken bone stitched close to her temple. Her veil and robes billowed around her bare feet. The woman untied the donkey and left the village, heading away along the path through the cotton fields. The child followed her.

* * *

By the light of a reddish moon just tipping over the horizon, the woman and her donkey made brisk progress. The child followed behind, keeping his distance and ducking aside when momentary patches of light in the sky threatened to reveal him. With every step the path became less distinct, yielding to the sand of the dunes and the ebb and flow of stones that appeared in successive waves. This brought them to the foot of a hill where the world seemed to come to an end.

Their shadows vanished. The child hurried on for fear of losing them but when he reached the top of the mound he froze. Below him glints of light flashed violently as if an entire army were being routed, and the sight filled his whole field of vision. This glittering stretched as far as he could see, and there was a feverish quality to its dazzling unpredictability.

The great river sprawled beneath the moon. It trundled its waters slowly, reluctantly towing with it the glints of light, as if dragging the memory of hopes that refused to abate. Along the ill-defined boundary between the river and the desert, the water was edged with long trails of salt, and endless carpets of stone woven from pure metal. The donkey waited on the bank while the woman filled the water containers tied to its flanks. Once her task was done she turned to face the river and launched into a long slow incantation. She lowered herself and stood back up, stretching out her arms to trace the path trodden by men, the path of their expectations, and finished by raising her arms to the stars and offering up her face to them for several long minutes.

Eventually the woman turned around and the child saw her face. Walking alongside the donkey, she started climbing up the bank to head back to the encampment. Droplets of water dripping from the containers gleamed in their tracks. When they reached the child, he hid behind a swell in the sand. The chill of the ground seeped through his thin clothes. He would have liked to stay there, melting into the ground, dissolving in the darkness, forgetting his sorrow and his fear. Not moving a muscle. As motionless as that barely breathing body back there in the village, under the tenting . . . But he was just a child. When he got back to his feet he realized he was alone. He ran to catch up with the shadows. As he raced along, he fled his thoughts, and the speed sharpened the raw cold still on his skin.

Back at the village, the woman was drawing water from one of the containers. The child watched her carry it into the tent. He joined her, stepping into the tent and slipping back under the blanket, in the dark once more. But something had changed. There was a man crouching in one corner, a worn piece of cloth wound around his naked torso, and he was chanting monotonously, oblivious to the goings-on around him, rocking back and forth to the rhythm of his own voice. Every now and then his face appeared clearly when he leaned into the unreliable glow of lamplight, then it was swallowed by the semidarkness again. And yet it wasn't the strange sight of this old man swaying between the shadows and the light that struck the child. Before he'd even had a chance to see any of this, his heart was gripped by the mournful words of the old man's lament:

She went out like a fire
With no embers left to burn

2

The child understood the old man's words but his tears wouldn't fall. He would have liked to feel them roll over his cheeks, to rest in their warmth, to follow their progress from eyelid to lip and on down to his chin. But they stayed locked deep inside him. He felt strangely relieved, almost happy. He'd listened to the women coming and going all night. Now the waiting was at an end.

He went over to the darkest corner of the tent and sat on an undyed wool blanket. The stub of a candle shed its trembling light over the middle of the tent. From time to time chattering silhouettes walked past, briefly masking its unsteady flame, their long veils wafting haphazardly, reminding him of evenings filled with feasting and dancing.

The body had been laid out in the far corner of the tent, opposite him. But he couldn't see it properly because a fence of sunflowers had been erected around it to hide it. If he watched carefully, though, he could make out the women's busying hands as they poured water and moaned softly.

She went out like a fire
With no embers left to burn

The man carried on with his solitary droning. From where the child was sitting, he could now see the shadowy furrows cast by the candle flame between the man's eyebrows and the wool scarf tied around his forehead. He could see the old man's beard waving like a banner, his body unfailingly marking out the rhythm as he rocked.

She went out like a fire
With no embers left to burn

The endless lament filled the space. As he listened to it, allowed himself to be lulled by it, the child managed to forget the women's macabre bustling, even stopped hearing the splashes of the water they periodically sluiced over the body.

On summer nights when work in the fields had stopped, dogs roamed close to the houses, near where people were, hoping for some attention or tidbit. But they never had their own place by the fire. They were driven away, sometimes with stones, until, resigned, they settled not far from the sleeping sheep.

On those nights, people often gathered under a tent like this one. The men made themselves comfortable, folding their legs under them, and forming a square around the glowing embers in a fireplace. The women made tea, poured it into glasses, and put them on a tray which was passed from one man to the next. The constant hubbub of voices was sometimes smothered by the whistling wind that announced a storm. Then, out of nowhere, a long silence would settle over them. The storyteller had arrived. Making his way through the rows, he would sit in the middle, book in hand.

His deep voice, filled with sunlight and clamor, served up songs, unheard news, and smells from faraway places and people. The women stood in the shadows while the children peered through the tight rows of men, trying to make out the storyteller's face where they might read the reverberating depths of the stories they were listening to.

The child loved these occasions. He too stood on tiptoe to peek through the shoulders and shawls. But he was still too small. Although he couldn't see, he could hear. He listened intently to tales of horsemen from lands whose names no one knew, men who traveled over deserts and plains, crossed rivers and seas, always courageous, always conquering, subjecting other men to their laws by the thousand, killing them by the hundred, and carrying their standards and their faith ever farther.

Sometimes the storyteller would flatter the head of the family playing host to him by giving the man's name to the hero, and the story would catch the child by surprise. It made his head spin: these familiar people, these men he came across on dusty paths every day, they were suddenly being credited with fantastic exploits! These people he knew, whose weaknesses he knew . . . and yet for now, for a moment, they became great warriors.

The following day, and for a few days after that, he would make a point of monitoring them, with a sort of respect mingled with suspicion. He hoped to catch them in mid-transformation and in a flash see them clothed in embroidered cloaks and flanked by huge black horses that they would mount and spur on toward the horizon in a single bound. He would spend hours like that, watching them, waiting for—and also dreading—the miracle. But the miracle never came and he ended up doubting there was any magic at all.

Over in the far corner, the man's voice grew shrill, waking the child from his reverie. The boy shifted, drawing his legs up to his chest and rolling himself up in the blanket, hugging his tightly crossed arms to his chest. A pleasant sensation tingled the tips of his fingers, a feeling as sweet as the one that had swept through him when that other hand had reached for his and brushed over it gently. The hand he would never feel again.

3

His mother had called him over.

"Come on, come here."

He hardly slept at all now that she was ill. People came to see her, exchanged a few words with her. But she tired quickly. When they left, they lingered outside the tent, chatting. They never referred to the illness, hardly even mentioned it, and talked in the past tense: "She had a sad life."

A sad life! They talked about it as if it was inevitable. Which is why the child didn't resent them for it. But the grandmother never disguised her rancor and this upset him. What did her complaining matter when he could see his mother was dying? Yes, his grandmother had done everything for her daughter. Yes, she had managed to find the best possible match for her, a man from the neighboring village, the only one with a solid house of bricks and mortar, standing facing the tents covered with "cob," sun-dried earth reinforced with straw. A man who had the only radio in the region, and even a truck. Yes, she'd succeeded in putting her daughter forward, and this despite the hostility of a first wife with whom the man already had three children. But no, it wasn't true, his mother hadn't been ungrateful because she'd failed to keep this lucky match. No, his grandmother shouldn't criticize her for being driven away and for coming home with only one of the two children she had from the marriage.

Surely everyone in the village knew the match had been based entirely on the grandmother's self-interest? Was there anyone who didn't know she'd arranged it with the sole aim of showing off and being feared and respected? Besides, she hadn't lost any time before trying to marry her daughter off again. But she hadn't found anyone with enough land and a big enough flock; the few remaining possible husbands had refused to take a woman who'd already been repudiated. They knew perfectly well her repudiation had no basis—other than the jealousy and scheming of the other wife, who'd eventually won her husband over. But whatever the reason, a repudiated woman was a fallen woman. No one would want her.

In desperation, the grandmother had agreed to give her to a man from a similar background.

When the child's mother had remarried, he'd been left on his own, in his grandmother's care. He would sometimes accompany his young aunt when she fetched water with her donkey. But in the evenings, as the sun went down behind the hills, he lay awake in the dark and thought of his mother, far away, in a cob-walled house on the edge of the village.

He went to see her as often as he could. He'd realized she wasn't well. He'd never known her to be very strong: she'd fallen ill just after he was born. And then she'd had two children from her second marriage, a son and a daughter, and that had taken even more out of her.

But one time when he visited her, a grimace of pain had cast a deep shadow over her face.

"My stomach's hurting a bit," she'd said with a smile so as not to worry him. "I wish I could spread it out on the banks of the river like a djellaba, and wash it down with lots of water."

She screwed up her face again when she sat down. As time went by the pain grew worse, racking her stomach and making it difficult for her to talk for minutes on end. Then one day, she stayed in bed.

"Come on. Come here."

In the quiet of the night, dogs could be heard calling to each other in long anguished howls, from one flock to the next. In the middle of the tent, in a hearth dug out of the ground, straw and dried cotton crackled, throwing up sparks.

He'd gone over to her. She'd reached out her hand, trying to find his, and had turned to look at him. In her eyes he saw birds, and big white flowers bending to the wind, and cool shadows. He saw the memory of times when they used to talk to each other, when she would take him in her arms, a surprised little boy who didn't understand what she was doing. She'd looked deep into his eyes without a word, but oh, how much he'd read in her gaze! It was then that she brushed his hand with hers with aching gentleness. The child was so moved he started shaking. Then his mother's hand lolled slowly to the floor. She had fallen asleep.

He'd stayed by her side watching her for a long time, then slipped away without a sound. Outside, the sky was motionless, the stars frozen in place, shining for themselves alone; the wind had dropped; and the dogs had stopped yelping. The desert had no soul.

4

The child had never really believed the storytellers, never really accepted that someone could always win like the heroic soldiers in their tales. But he'd listened to them so often he'd eventually convinced himself that, if you fought, you could always hope. And now, as the women carried on weeping for his dead mother, he'd just discovered that even hope isn't always rewarded.

Movements in the darkness, fleeting shadows, the old man's keening, the lamp glimmering . . . it was all over now, propelled into the past. The sun had dissipated the anguish and the village was back to its usual occupations. There in the dust, a few devoted villagers were preparing the body. The child didn't feel it had anything to do with him. This certainly wasn't indifference, though. No, it was more that he seemed to be absent from the world. His hurts and ordeals bore down on his young shoulders and he was bending like a reed under the suffering.

* * *

When he was born his mother was just barely fifteen. No one had come to her bedside to soothe her. No woman from her village had made the trip to come and support her, to help her cope with the pain. No one had agreed to keep her company, to calm her fears or wash the newborn baby. She'd given birth alone. With no friend or relation. Already excluded thanks to the other woman's scheming.

When a shadow was eventually cast through the entrance to the tent, she thought her husband had come to see his son at last. Too weak to sit up, she managed only a tentative smile. It was him standing before her, but he seemed preoccupied and had a group of uneasy-looking men with him. Without looking at the baby, without even asking after him, without any kind words, he delivered his message. Seven times over he told her he no longer wanted her as a wife. Seven times over he threw a stone onto the beaten earth before the witnesses he'd summoned to escort him. He'd respected the rules. The child's mother was repudiated, forever. Just like that, for no reason.

Not one of the witnesses protested. And she kept quiet throughout the repudiation ritual. She didn't utter a single reproachful word. Didn't shed a single tear. She waited till her husband had gone; then, despite her weakened condition, she wrapped her veil around herself, swaddled her baby in a scarf, and left. Hunched over her child, exhausted, she walked away, slowly, painfully, every step an ordeal. For a long, long time people could still see her heading deeper into the desert.

She'd arrived at her mother's door on the point of collapse. But her mother didn't take her in. No. She stood barring the doorway, showering her daughter with insults and curses. Neighbors sidled over, inquisitive, snide. They showed no compassion, quite happy to watch the pale, wan young woman put her baby to the breast while the grandmother railed at her. No, not one neighbor reached out a hand to her.

When the miserable cortege set off, the child stayed behind. He didn't want to be involved in a funeral ceremony held by people who'd never shown any affection for his mother. He did look around for his brother, but couldn't see him. Perhaps fear had kept him at home in his father's house. The body was wrapped in white and laid on a bier of woven saplings, and a team of men lifted this onto their shoulders. They headed up the procession. Behind them came a few women, uttering the occasional desultory ritual lamentation. Farther behind, a man brought up the rear, unconvincingly intoning prayers for the dead.

The cortege cut across the fields where the brown cotton stalks shivered in the November wind. It stopped several times so the men could change places. The body was a burden to them. The child followed, hanging back. Then the fields disappeared and all that was left was a hill, clearly defined against the hard sky.

In the distance, the child could see the hole that had been dug in the sand. In the distance, he could still hear the women's cries and the muted litany of prayers. But none of it meant anything to him. Or rather, he preferred not to think about it. The white figure was lowered. It was laid on a plank which, in keeping with custom, was lowered to the bottom of the hole, then covered with sand. Even from far away, he could hear sand being thrown onto the body. The ceremony came to an end abruptly, like a job done, and the people dispersed.

It was only when he was alone that the child dared venture closer. The disturbed sand around the grave made a darker shape. All around it, hillocks of sand crumbled slowly. Apart from that, nothing, no one, just the wind.

When he came back, years later, the wind had swept the hillside bare.

5

"There were once many tribes living south of the river. They had horses, and they erected tents for the night and moved on to the rhythm of their flocks' search for new outcrops of sparse grass. Sometimes the tribes would gather together to shelter from the lacerating cold at night, or from the violent rains that fell for several hours, redecorating the hills with green. Then their tents made a sort of village in the middle of the desert, a village no traveler could see.

"All through the centuries, we, the Badawi—the Bedouins, as outsiders call us—have traveled the desert. We had to fight the sedentary peoples who claimed the lands we ventured across. All through the centuries they tried to rob us of these lands. But all through the centuries, our fathers managed to defend them.

"Times changed. The sedentary peoples grew powerful, their attacks more frequent. We had to settle down in order to challenge them, to protect ourselves. At first our tents stayed at the same encampment for months on end. Then, although no one meant or wanted this to happen, they stopped moving.

"Time was when we transported goods from one end of the desert to the other as we traveled with our flocks. We alone knew how, we alone could withstand the desert. Time was when we were accompanied by real caravanserai, hundreds of laden camels, and we journeyed back and forth across the land, from the cold mountains in the east to the sea in the west. Then, with the advent of trucks . . ."

The child stopped listening and looked around. In the half-light, on the walls of the tent, he could see the heavy goat-hair cloth straining against the wooden pegs stretching it into shape. Outside, where the air quivered in the heat, he could make out the silhouette of a tired horse shaking its head at regular intervals to drive away the flies. The hens scratching around it scattered and clucked every time it shook.

Beside the child, the old man was still talking, his eyes half closed, absorbed in the mists of memory. The boy was growing bored. As if realizing this, the old man suddenly changed what he was saying:

"You are a Badawi. Like your father and your father's father, and all those who traveled the desert before them. If you don't listen to your history, you'll be as light as a cloud in the sky, you'll never be able to settle, light as a feather carried away on the wind."

The old man paused, scratching at the ground as if hoping it would provide proof of what he was saying.

"Houses like your grandmother's," he went on, "were origi-
nally tents. In the past, our tents made big dark shapes against
the sand dunes. Then we reinforced their walls with woven straw
and onto that we put wet clay or mud mixed with cotton tufts,
which hardened as it dried. They now look like simple houses,
you can't tell them from the others. They've taken on the color
of the earth, of the desert . . ."

"Did you go to school?" the child interrupted.

"I learned to read, write, and count," the old man replied,
pretending to ignore the impropriety of the interruption. "But
I stopped going when I had to start work."

"Do you think children *should* go to school?"

"Why do you ask?"

"My grandmother doesn't want me to go," the child said
glumly.

"You should listen to her. She only wants what's best for
you."

"It's not fair!"

The old man gave a long sigh. "It'll be many years before
you know what's fair. Respecting your family, now, that's fair."

The child stood up. What did he care how things worked
in the past, what did he care about this family that fate had
snatched away from him?

"It's not fair!" he cried. "I say it's not fair and I stand by
that."

6

When the older children talked about school they became all mysterious, as if discussing some great secret. Listening from some way away, the child could hear what they were saying. He'd certainly tried to learn more about it, but every time he'd made as if to get any closer, the others had fallen silent. And then there were those peculiar symbols they drew on pieces of paper. Symbols that were somehow messages, but he couldn't decipher them.

He was intrigued by these enigmas for a long time, and then it occurred to him that he too could go to school. He told his grandmother this was what he wanted, but she wouldn't hear of it. She refused to listen to any explanations. He wouldn't be going to school. He had to make himself useful, earn the right to be under her roof. He'd learn his trade as a shepherd.

The school was several kilometers away and, more significantly, it was in the village where his father lived. Barriers enough for the grandmother to hope the child would be put off. But every morning he could hear children laughing as they headed for school. Every morning he stood by the door, watching them walk away, and every morning his longing to go with them grew stronger.

And so one morning he waited for the bustle to die down, slowly pushed aside the blankets so as not to wake his grandmother, lifted the canvas from across the doorway with infinite care, and slipped out, quick as a desert fox. He could see the other children's cheerful outlines already far ahead among the cotton plants. He set off, struggling to keep up with them. He was slowed by legs too short to match their pace and by his efforts to stay hidden. To follow without being caught. An art he'd mastered long ago. It was a bumpy path of sand and stone, and his bare feet hurt. He tripped several times, and occasionally had to run to keep sight of the tiny, distant cluster of schoolchildren in the sunlight. He followed it for a whole hour.

At last they reached the village. He stopped before the last turn in the track and stood on tiptoe to watch. The schoolchildren had gathered outside a house just like all the others, and had quietly arranged themselves in a neat group. They stood upright and quiet, waiting, their chatter and laughter silenced. The only sound in the morning air was an eagle's cry, way up in the sky.

Then a man appeared, walking toward them along the track, tall, stiff, his chest held high. He went over to a flagpole outside the house that the pupils were facing, and when he reached it,

the children sang the national anthem. The man proudly took
the rope and raised the flag, pulling powerfully and solemnly.
A black and a red stripe framing two green stars fluttered in the
flush of morning light. His duty done, the man walked away and
the children went through the doorway.

The child knew the man. He was his own father.

The children disappeared one after the other, swallowed up by
the dark opening, and the child waited a while. When no one
came back out, he thought this must be some secret entrance
and from here a path would lead to the school as he'd pictured
it, a palace with a wealth of fountains and gardens. He hesitated
for a moment before heading for the passageway himself.

As he walked toward it he heard a man's powerful voice
through the wall. His stomach constricted with fear. Was there
someone guarding the passageway? He risked a quick look
though a hole near the foot of the wall, where the cob had bro-
ken away under the scorching sun. What he saw came as more
of a shock than the booming voice reverberating in his ears. On
the far side of the wall there was just a single room, exactly like
the one in his grandmother's house: square and white, with bare
walls. Was this the school? But where was the palace, and where
were the gardens? He was so disappointed he almost turned tail,
fled, ran home, and gave up the idea. But he checked himself;
he didn't want to back down. He leaned a little closer to see the
room as best he could from where he was. Nailed to one wall
was a painting of a plant greener, brighter, and more luxuriant
than any he'd ever seen in his life. This reassured him. Even in
that plain, bare room there were wonders!

He could now also see the pupils sitting in silent rows. To the right of the painting a stern-looking man was brandishing a long cane, beating the hands of a contrite boy.

"If you don't bring any firewood for the school tomorrow, you'll have a double punishment," the man said.

Some of the pupils laughed at their scolded classmate. The child watching wasn't surprised: he knew how spiteful they could be. He stayed watching for a long time, then, for fear of being caught, eventually decided he should leave. On the way home he promised himself he would find out more. But he'd only just come in sight of the village when he spotted his grandmother's yellow headscarf bobbing agitatedly outside her house. When he appeared she launched herself at him.

"I've looked everywhere for you! You'll be the death of me—just like your mother."

He flinched, then stared so intently at his grandmother that she froze, openmouthed. Making the most of her astonishment, he walked on past her and continued on his way, unhurried and indifferent to the shrieking that started up again behind him. He stayed away the whole day and came home only in the evening. Of course he was punished. He was sent to bed without so much as a mouthful of mutton. It didn't matter. He was looking forward to morning.

7

The child had made up his mind and knew what he had to do. He just had to take the step . . . but perhaps that was the hardest part. The following day he went to the next village again and spent the morning at the foot of the school wall, listening to what was being said inside. When the teacher announced it was time for lunch, he stood up and took himself home. He hadn't had the courage to go in. He spent a week like this, wandering around outside the classroom but not daring to go in.

His grandmother screamed at him again, and he stood up to her.

"If you won't let me go, I'll ask our neighbors if I can live with them," he said.

She glowered at him.

"Oh yes, you have it in you to shame me like that in front of everyone!"

Eventually she stopped her recriminations. The child's afternoons were set to the rhythms of the flock, and he allowed his courage to ripen.

Today was the big day. He brought, rolled up in a piece of canvas, a few things he'd gathered together on the sly: a worn pencil, some sheets of paper, and a cloth. He had gotten up before anyone else, even before the exuberant group of schoolchildren passed. When the other children arrived at school, they found him sitting outside. Although they were all barefoot, they had new clothes and shiny satchels while he had only his djellaba and his piece of canvas.

When they saw the little new boy, the schoolchildren clustered around him, laughing, jostling him, and making fun of his djellaba. At first the child felt something like the burrow of a desert fox opening up in his stomach, then a cold feeling seeped inside him. He looked around but found not one friendly face, not one sign of understanding. In the end, his shame made him break out of the hostile circle. Distraught, he went and stood some distance away on the path, in the irrational hope of seeing his brother appear, the brother who'd been kept at home by his father. *He* would defend him, the child thought; he would console him. But the path was empty.

The teacher had heard the commotion and came outside. He saw the child standing on his own and went over to him.

"What's your name?" he asked.

"Maïouf."

"Why aren't you with the others?"

"I'm waiting for my brother."

* * *

The teacher studied the child's pale face, his worn djellaba, and the belongings he'd awkwardly scraped back together after the other boys scattered them. Without a word, the teacher took his hand and turned back toward the others, who fell silent.

"Stand in proper rows!" he barked. "It's my job to look after new pupils. I don't want to hear any more comments about him."

Maïouf didn't see his brother that day. He later learned that his father's wife didn't want him going back to school now. But Maïouf himself was impatient to learn. In the evenings, to avoid his grandmother's reprimands, he stayed behind in the cotton fields to do his homework, copying out the letters and numerals that the teacher had written on the blackboard.

Days went by. The first nip of cold was in the air. In the mornings bare feet could stick to the frosty ground, and the children had to run to get to school without freezing. Maïouf was soon making good progress. But the other children struggled to accept that this poor kid, the son of a repudiated woman, was their equal; and worse than that: he was a better student than any of them.

One afternoon while the teacher was handing back homework, he congratulated Maïouf: he had achieved the best grade.

"You work hard. I'm proud of you. You don't need to bring any firewood tomorrow."

When the lesson was over all the children put their things into their satchels. The teacher said good-bye and they were free to leave. Maïouf was happy. He felt full of courage, ready—if need be—to cope with his grandmother's ranting when he arrived

home. He could already picture himself telling her how his hard
work had paid off.

"Oh, and now you're proud to be a layabout!" was all she
said.

What did he care?

Lost in his thoughts, Maïouf didn't hear the others come over to
him. In a flash someone grabbed his arms, his head was covered
with a rag, and he was dragged off the path. He couldn't see
anything, but he could tell from the crunch of sand under his
feet that he was being taken toward the desert. He struggled to
break free, tried to scream.

His voice was stifled by the rag. The only sound he could
hear was his own breathing. Then one of the boys holding
him started laughing. It was a laugh loaded with spite. Now he
thought he understood and struggled again.

"Leave me alone!" he bellowed.

He could hear them digging in the sand. Someone gave
him a sudden shove, and he toppled forward. He was in a hole
in the ground, and only just had time to roll over before the
sand was being thrown onto him. Soon he was buried—sand
everywhere! Weighing down on him, percolating through the
cloth, into his nose, his eyes, his ears, and his mouth. There was
another cruel laugh.

"That'll teach you to be friends with the teacher!" said a
voice.

Then silence. Paralyzed in the hole, imprisoned by the
sand, with the hood still over his head, Maïouf waited, though
he didn't know what for. For the nasty prank to end, perhaps,

for someone to come and get him out. But no one came and he started to suffocate. The blood roared in his temples, stars danced like butterflies before his unseeing eyes. He was close to passing out.

With a surge of fury and boundless sadness he stiffened his whole body like a blade. And just as he'd given up hope, the sand opened. He hauled himself up in the trench, freed his arms, pulled himself out, rolled onto his side, and then pulled off the rag at last. It was only after he'd greedily taken several deep breaths and cleared the sand from his mouth and nose that he looked around. He was alone.

The empty desert was filling with shadows. A fox's cry rang out far in the distance.

It was dark by the time Maïouf pulled aside the canvas doorway. He hardly heard the scolding and threw himself onto his bed.

From now on, he promised himself, he'd be the best.

8

The truck had pride of place in the middle of the yard. It was an American truck with a wide trailer which could transport hundreds of liters of water, dozens of sheep, and even people. When it passed it made such a noise and raised so much dust that people scattered in its path. And yet everyone was envious of that truck.

School was over, but there was still one thing Maïouf had to do. Something he did with far less enthusiasm than his homework. Since he'd been attending school, his father had taken to summoning him. And every time his father requested his presence, Maïouf was anxious. He didn't know how to behave or even what to say, and still less why he had to go at all, unless it was only to be humiliated. All his father seemed to want from these "interviews" was to prove he was boss.

* * *

The child walked across the yard, giving the truck a respectful berth, climbed the few steps to the narrow veranda that ran the length of the house, wiped the dust from his feet, and called out. No one replied. He walked through the doorless opening.

His father was sitting amid piles of soft cushions, deep in conversation. Still talking, he gestured brusquely toward the far end of the room. Maïouf went to sit not far from one of the shiny copper oil lamps that were his father's pride and joy. Later, when night fell, he would get up and tend to the lamp. He never let anyone light it for him. It was his job to provide light, to show that you could see clearly in his house, without the heavy smell of candle stubs floating in mutton fat and shedding a feeble shaky glow. Then his older sons would come in carrying other lamps which the father would light ceremoniously, and they would head off in procession toward other rooms in the house. They would set the lamps down around the place and leave them burning until bedtime.

Maïouf sat waiting. Every now and then the door opened, and a new visitor came in to have a cup of tea with his father, or ask for his advice, his guidance. No one greeted Maïouf, no one even noticed him. The coming and going carried on, and Maïouf sat in the room as if he didn't exist, as if he were invisible to them. After what felt like an eternity, he summoned his courage and dared to ask for permission to leave. When his father didn't reply he started to get to his feet.

"I didn't say you could go!" His voice snapped like a whip.

* * *

Maïouf stayed frozen to the spot. The conversation that had been droning on for hours was over. His father looked at him.

"I hear you've honored me at school. Good. You can go. But come back tomorrow." Now that he'd spoken, the father turned back to his guest with a smile. Just as Maïouf was about to walk through the doorway, though, he called, "Don't forget, I said tomorrow."

It was cool outside in the shadow of the veranda. Maïouf hovered for a moment. The women were preparing a meal inside, and he knew his stepmother was there; he could hear her voice. In the end he turned and left. He could have stayed hidden in the shade of the awning over the veranda but he could feel the gray, windowless bulk of the house behind him. It drove him away. He'd never liked that block of cement. It was a huge, perfectly symmetrical one-story building. It had one entrance at the front and one at the back but there were no windows on these elevations. The windows were on the other two sides. A house like this probably indicated great wealth but, as far as Maïouf was concerned, all it represented was ugliness. He walked around this cube and went up the outside staircase that ran along one wall. He arrived on the roof, which had been turned into a terrace. And that's where he sat down. All he had to do now was wait for his aunt to come past. She wouldn't be long, she and her donkey with the water containers bouncing to the rhythm of its footfalls.

The sun was going down when he saw her at last. She was walking toward the house, surrounded by a halo of dust raised by the donkey. The water containers bobbed against the animal's flanks. On the trip back from the river they wouldn't move about as they did now, and the donkey would be less frisky, treading slowly, crushed by the weight.

Maïouf sat up, instantly happy. His aunt and the donkey walked past, pretending to ignore him, and he had to run to catch up with them. As soon as they were out of sight of the house, his aunt turned and took him in her arms.

"Did you have a good day?" she asked, smiling.

"Just normal."

"Will you help me fill these up?"

When they reached the riverbank, they went to a sheltered creek where the water ran clear and you could even see fish darting about. They filled the containers, and the drips shone like pearls in the light of the setting sun.

9

Their teacher was going back to the city. That was how it worked. Every year the school took on a different schoolmaster.

As was the custom, the children had gathered outside the school to wait for their teacher and walk him to his bus. They were prepared for a real expedition: it was several kilometers from the village to the main road; then, once there, they would have to wait, and the waiting could go on for hours. Everyone knew the bus would pass along that road, yes. But at what time, no one could say. Not that anyone complained; waiting was an ingrained habit here, hours were much less important than seasons.

The teacher came out of the small house he'd been allocated for the year. Maïouf thought he looked a bit emotional . . . unless it was Maïouf himself who was emotional to see his first teacher leave.

The little posse set off. They had to walk across fields and take running jumps over the irrigation ditches. Maïouf stayed close to the teacher but as they cleared one of the ditches he stopped in amazement: the teacher had just jumped and carried on walking but there, hidden by the leaves of a watermelon, lay gleaming colored pencils and a ruler which had slipped out of his bag. Nice shiny, well-sharpened pencils. A red one, a blue one, and a black one; and the ruler, the only one they'd had in the classroom! All that the other children could think of was messing about, and they hadn't noticed anything. In fact, they'd already caught up with the teacher, who was setting quite a pace. Alone at the back, Maïouf hesitated, then bent down and picked up the ruler and crayons, and hid them in a fold of his djellaba before running to catch up with the rest of the group forging ahead in the sunshine.

When they reached the road it was deserted. Two hours trickled by, two hours through which Maïouf clutched his precious prize to him. Then the green dot of the bus appeared on the horizon, and the teacher called his pupils together. He said good-bye to them, addressing them each individually and saying a solemn farewell. He only just had time to finish as the bus stopped. He was about to climb in when Maïouf stepped up to him and thrust the ruler and pencils at him. The teacher took them without a word, his eyes shining, then he leaned toward the child and handed them back to him.

"I went barefoot too once," he said quietly.

Through the clouds of dust raised by the bus, Maïouf thought he could see a hand waving to him in the rear window.

* * *

Time went by. Maïouf grew. His grandmother had long since
given up trying to run his life. She didn't accept the situation,
oh no . . . She'd never been able to bear the fact that he went to
school. A chilly indifference had been established between them.

Thanks to school, Maïouf's horizons had expanded further than
the eye could see. He'd kept the promise he'd made to himself
the day his classmates buried him in the sand and tried to break
his will: he was top of the class. This had allowed him to carry
on with his education even though, after the first few years, he
had to move to another school which meant going to a different
village, even farther away. Luckily, Maïouf had found himself a
companion for the journey: his grandmother's youngest son,
whom he had secretly taught to read, write, and count, followed
him to school every day, claiming he was going to tend the flocks.

His new school was different. It may not have been the
palace he'd naively dreamed of, but at least it was no longer the
simple cob shack he'd left behind. This school building was
white, welcoming, solid. The village was also different from those
he'd known so far. Maïouf was impressed by its brick houses,
bigger and taller than his grandmother's house, taller even than
his father's; some of them looked like tents piled onto each other
with rooms on top of others.

In this village he'd come to understand the word "shop."
How many times had he heard that word without being able to
give it any substance, to picture it? Until now, his only concept of
a shop was the *hawage*, the peddler who came through from time

to time with his two donkeys laden with wares. He now knew it was a place where people waited all day long. He'd also had a chance to see a well where the water spouted out miraculously when you operated the pulley.

But none of that had meant much compared with what this modest building could promise him: learning. Now he was going to learn.

10

The morning air was still cool when the bus stopped in a square bustling with people. Nobody paid any attention to the children getting out. People wearing strange clothes, like those in pictures in geography books, hurried in every direction, not bothering to say hello or smile. Maïouf felt intimidated; he ventured a few greetings but no one responded. Afraid he was making some blunder in this world with its unfamiliar rules, he clung still closer to the group of schoolchildren, following as soon as they set off.

He'd reached the end of middle school, and now here he was in a big town, taking his *brevet* exam to get into senior school. As he walked with the other children he gazed inquisitively at the city; it had been no more than a myth only yesterday. He looked at the square lined with trees and flowers, and the wide avenues leading away from it. Between the trees he could also see lawns with not a single sheep sauntering across them. Is this what the palaces were like in the storytellers' tales?

He was woken from his daydreaming by the deafening hubbub coming from the playground of the school where the exam was being held. Hundreds of schoolchildren from all over the region were gathered, laughing and shouting, and they all seemed to know each other. A wave of despair washed over Maïouf. He'd never pass. What good was all that work if he was to fail here, so close to his goal? But he didn't have time to give in to his fears. Stern-looking men had arrived and were already dividing the sea of suddenly silent children into small groups. Maïouf had no choice but to go with the flow. Before entering the building he was subjected to a thorough frisking, then—heart thumping—he stepped into the exam hall.

The pupils were asked to sit down, each at an individual desk; then their candidate identity forms were handed out. Maïouf had managed to get hold of a pen, and he took it out now with a sense of occasion. When he unscrewed the lid a long dribble of ink leaked over his fingers. He stood up, horrified, looking for a rag, anything to wipe his hand and not mark the precious exam paper. In his consternation he hadn't noticed that the exam supervisors had come into the room. He realized only when he felt someone take hold of his arm. A painful memory flashed through his mind and he spun around in terror.

A strange calm spread through him, the calm of autumn days when the sky opens up to reveal the sun after a sandstorm. Standing smiling in front of him was *the* teacher, his first teacher.

"I'm proud to see you here," the man whispered. "What luck, I'm the invigilator in the room where you're taking your exam."

Maïouf was speechless with surprise. It was only then that his former teacher looked down and saw his spattered hands. Without another word, he leaned forward, took a cloth that was hanging on the wall, handed it to Maïouf, and walked away.

Maïouf passed his *brevet*.

It should have been big news, celebrated in style. His young uncle showed how happy he was by coming to greet him as he stepped off the bus. Dusk was falling over the desert, it was the time of day when they brought the animals in, but he'd managed to get here and wait for Maïouf without anyone realizing. They walked back to the village side by side, happy to be together again, his young uncle shooting him admiring looks. As they walked they came across Maïouf's aunt on her way back from the river. When she saw him, she let go of the donkey's bridle, ran over to him, and threw her arms around his neck, kissing him and laughing, as she always had.

But when he reached the village, when he stood before his grandmother's house, he was met by only a blank stare. The same stare his father would give him, showing no hint of satisfaction, not an ounce of pride. As for his stepmother, all she would do was display her irritation, struggling to accept that the second wife's son had succeeded. It was early evening and the houses in the village glowed red in the light of the setting sun. Maïouf had always liked this time of day, this in-between time when people switched from one activity to another but didn't know exactly what stage the sun had reached in its descent. And yet, on that particular day, those glowing colors sidling down the walls looked sinister to him.

* * *

Having gulped down his evening meal, Maïouf stood in the doorway listening with a heavy heart to the music and singing coming from the homes of other successful candidates. Some families had sacrificed lambs to honor their children's success, and he'd smelled the aroma of roasting lamb earlier; it had been hanging over the village when he arrived. He didn't spend long on this bitter pleasure, but as he lay down to sleep late that night, he heard gunshots fired into the sky, the crowning moment of the celebrations. He turned over in his bed and tried not to think about all this; it had nothing to do with him.

The only senior school in the area was in Raqqa, the regional capital. Another change lay ahead, another new school for Maïouf, still farther from the village. It was too far to make the journey every day so he would have to move there. But he was only twelve; he had hardly any money; and, judging by the indifference everyone had shown him, he couldn't imagine being helped, not in any way. Perhaps that's what made him stronger.

11

When Maïouf arrived in Raqqa a few weeks before the beginning of the term he had no trouble making up his mind to confront what was a strange new problem for him: finding accommodations. Not that he saw this as especially momentous; he'd run into so many difficulties all his life, had to fight so much adversity, that finding accommodations in an unfamiliar city didn't strike him as any different, just another problem to solve. Nothing to fret about.

Until now Maïouf had lived in his grandmother's house, true, but that house had never been his home. Even the village where he'd grown up had never been home. He hadn't chosen to be excluded from it, but he'd always felt rejected. He'd always felt he was on the margins of the life going on around him. The son of a dead, repudiated woman. Poor, despite who his father was. Had he made friends? Very few. None if you didn't count his aunt and his young uncle. At the end of the day, nothing and no one tied him to the place. Perhaps the desert. But the desert was something you had to fight against, to master. A facet of fate. So moving to Raqqa was no upheaval for him, he just had to find somewhere to live.

Aged all of twelve, then, Maïouf alighted from the bus that had brought him to the city, more concerned about his new school than the thought of putting a roof over his head. The city sprawling before him didn't succeed in securing his attention. All that activity; those streets heading off into an inextricable, hopelessly impenetrable labyrinth; that bustle; that fizzing of colors, noises, and faces; the lack of a horizon, of any distance . . . it all felt so artificial to him that it was like being in a flimsy dream, too insubstantial to distract him from his concerns. The moment he set foot on the beaten earth of the ground he went about finding somewhere to live. He'd been given a few addresses, and found them with the help of passersby. One of them would fit the bill. With his childish assumptions about his own entitlement, Maïouf wasn't even surprised when he was offered a bed by a man who earned a living from his humble horse-drawn taxi and delivery service. There was nothing extraordinary about this invitation; hospitality was a tradition in Raqqa, a favor like any other, even if there was a connection between Maïouf's father's name and the speed with which he found accommodations.

What mattered to him was school; a roof and a bed were necessities. He followed his host's wife as she led him to the small room he'd been allocated. He set down his belongings, asked for a glass of water, and sat on the iron bed that would be his for the next few years.

*   *   *

Maïouf hadn't grown up in opulent surroundings so this bed, the bread his host's wife gave him every day, and the occasional meals he was given by his classmates' families were enough to meet his hopes and needs. He quickly got used to the city, and he enjoyed his route to school. It took him down tiny streets, and when he came out onto the main square with its impressive clock tower he felt very proud to be crossing it confidently. Then he went down a long avenue lined with scrawny trees before reaching the school gates.

He had to push himself at school, and often had to work late into the night to catch up with the others. It wasn't that his previous schoolmasters had been bad teachers, but he was from the desert, a Badawi, and the other boys in his class were from much bigger villages than his or small towns or even, in some cases, from Raqqa.

12

The couple who gave him accommodations had two daughters. One of these girls produced indefinable feelings in Maïouf every time he came across her. They'd meet and exchange a few words but their relationship never seemed to go beyond being polite, courteous. But oh, how often Maïouf thought of her!

In Raqqa, as in the rest of the country, cinemas were open-air. If you knew someone whose windows looked out over the square where the screen was set up, you could watch a screening without spending any money. One of Maïouf's school friends had just this luck, and Maïouf had taken advantage of it once or twice. Those moving images from a different world had come as a shock to him, but he was soon captivated by them.

With this advantage up his sleeve, it occurred to him one day that he could invite the daughter of the house to share the pleasure. At least, he thought, it would give him an opportunity to talk to her beyond social niceties. So one afternoon, thinking she might be in the kitchen, he strolled into the room casually. She was there, as he'd expected, and she was alone. He greeted her as he came in, walked past her, and pretended to look for something in the drawers, trying frantically to summon the courage to talk to her. Eventually, without meeting her eye, he mumbled that he could, if she wanted, invite her for the evening to, well, to watch a film, because he had a friend . . . To his enormous relief, she understood what he meant and, more important, said yes.

They were showing a romantic film that evening. The girl had followed Maïouf all the way to his friend's apartment without saying a word. Now sitting with her on one side and his friend on the other, Maïouf was a jumble of emotions. It was a pleasure feeling the girl's warmth beside him, but the pleasure was tempered with fear. He felt so awkward! Of course, on the inside, he was incredibly proud to have brought an actual girl to his friend's place. But at the same time, as is often the case in these situations, he desperately wanted to be somewhere else. So much so that he felt impatient, even anxious, for the film to start just so he'd have something to do.

With the very opening shots of the film he completely surrendered to it. All through the screening he had eyes only for the heroine, forgetting the girl he'd brought with him. She was interested only in what was happening on-screen, anyway. When the screen finally fell dark and people stood up to leave, Maïouf sat up. He noticed that the girl had mimicked this move, as if they were in unison. After drinking the cup of mint tea made by his friend's mother, and thanking his friend for his hospitality, he took the young girl back to her house, which, for this year,

was his home too. He did it without thinking of the implications because he was lost in his thoughts, haunted by images
from the film. He walked her home in silence, and left her with
a simple nod of his head which could have meant thank you or
good night. When he was working away at his books as usual
the following day, Maïouf felt rather than saw the canvas across
his doorway sway and then move slowly aside.

The girl came in, let the canvas drop back gently, and leaned
against the wall without a word. Maïouf sat there paralyzed with
fear and emotion. Their outing the previous evening had calmed
his longing, and he may have pictured others in the future, but
hadn't envisaged going beyond that. He hadn't anticipated that
she might . . . His head was bombarded by the most incongru-
ous ideas. He thought of one of his friends' brothers who was
in bed with bronchitis because he'd hidden in a vat full of water
when the father of the girl he was with came home unexpect-
edly. He thought of the tragedy that had happened a few days
earlier when a young girl from a neighboring house had died at
the hands of an abortionist. He also remembered the strict rules
that govern relations between girls and boys, the intransigent
pride of his people, and the tragic tales of love he'd heard. And
it all paralyzed him.

After an interminable silence, the girl lifted the canvas once
more and was gone.

13

Maïouf had now been living in Raqqa for two years, and over that time while he'd been completely devoted to his studies, he felt he'd changed families, changed worlds. He'd been back to the village very little; what did it have to offer him? If he wanted to get the full flavor of the desert, he need only get outside the city and walk a few steps. But as time went by he'd felt this need less and less. He wasn't really a city boy, but neither was he entirely a desert dweller as his "brothers" were when they headed off into the dunes to tend to their flocks. Neither one nor the other, he felt that his only anchor, besides school, was the house where he slept. One Thursday as he walked through the front door of this house, he was greeted by an unusual buzz of activity. His host's wife wouldn't tell him anything, but an hour later, when he was finishing some homework, he heard the sputtering roar of a big vehicle stopping outside the house. It was his father's truck, he'd have recognized it just from the sound of its engine.

The dust swirling around it seeped in through the shutters to confirm the fact, if there was any doubt. What was it doing here? Maïouf hardly had time to grab a few things. The driver waiting for him was showing signs of impatience, and Maïouf had barely climbed in beside him before the man threw the truck back into gear.

They drove along the main road for a long time. After crossing a desert landscape whose uneven road surface added to the truck's lurching and forced Maïouf to cling to the dilapidated seat, they came to a halt in the yard of his father's house. But it wasn't his father who came to greet him when he jumped from the running board, his body still thrumming with the vibrations of the journey. It was his stepmother, followed by his sister and a young woman—a rather pretty young woman—hanging back behind the other two women.

Maïouf rubbed his face as his stepmother came and stood squarely before him. No two ways about it, she was a good-looking woman. Her smooth skin, the clean lines of her face, and her long dark hair exuded a powerful energy. He'd always found her striking but he didn't like her. Wasn't she responsible for his mother's repudiation, with her scheming, the pressure she'd put on everyone around her, and her spiteful jealousy which had eventually won the day? Here she was now, dressed, as usual, in bright colors, her eyes edged with kohl and her hair hennaed, an imposing figure standing imperiously in front of his father's house.

"You're over fourteen now," she announced, without even saying hello. "It's high time you thought of finding yourself a wife. You need to become a man. Boys your age are already married here. Just because you live in Raqqa you don't have to be an exception. If you stay unmarried you'll bring shame on the family."

Maïouf was so surprised by her tirade he stood rooted to the spot. Thinking she'd finished, he opened his mouth to speak but didn't have time to say a word. His stepmother had already turned to the girl waiting meekly behind her and, waving a hand in her direction, added, "Here's the girl you're going to marry. She's my niece. Your father's agreed to it."

The sun scorched Maïouf's face and he'd have been more comfortable quenching his thirst and washing his mouth, his eyes, and the back of his neck after his journey, rather than being confronted with the prospect of marriage.

He took a step back so he could gather his wits but also to shelter in the shade of the truck. The strong smell of grease and diesel from the hot engine was somehow reassuring, tangible, a protest against the ethereal image of his stepmother shimmering in the heat haze that rose from the ground. It was an unpleasant, awkward situation. No one had asked how he felt. It hadn't even occurred to anyone that he might refuse to cooperate.

If he did refuse, if he expressed an opinion, a response, things could get nasty. His mother's fate was proof enough of his father's violent reactions and his stepmother's frighteningly vindictive nature. But agreeing to this meant abandoning his independence and his studies, and submitting to the will of this woman he loathed. The girl was pretty, yes, but she was at least ten years older than Maïouf. She was probably not responsible for what was happening, but he couldn't imagine spending his life with her. How could he control a woman ten years older than himself?

*   *   *

He made his own decision very swiftly: without explicitly saying no, he would do everything he could to stop this marriage. So he politely expressed his thanks for the offer that had been made to him and said he would think about it but he had work that needed finishing and wondered whether the truck could take him back to Raqqa. Once back in the city, he hoped he'd find other ways of deferring this arrangement.

This ambiguous reaction provoked a distinct chill. His stepmother seemed to want to say something else, perhaps to keep him there, but decided against it and simply nodded at the driver, who climbed back into the truck. Maïouf didn't say another word but he too jumped up onto the front seat and looked determinedly out toward the desert. The truck rumbled to life, reversed around the yard, and set off, much to Maïouf's relief.

Maïouf was lucky in this business: sometime after he returned to Raqqa, when he was still waiting anxiously to hear how his father had reacted, he gathered that his intended bride had herself shown signs of resistance. She was ambitious and knew he would be entitled to only a paltry share of the inheritance. And, anyway, he was a student, not something she viewed as an honorable activity, or at least not an activity for a man, a true man, the sort who drives sheep, or trucks. Then there was the fact that Maïouf had asked for time to consider the question . . . and she'd decided to interpret this as a no, and—to his great relief—she'd told him that, as he renounced his promise to marry her, she accepted his decision. Now all that remained was to undo what the stepmother had arranged, in other words to release both parties from their promises.

In desert villages, marriages are usually decided by the *mukhtar*, the head of the village. He concludes arrangements, whether confirming or revoking promises. He is the supreme judge and no one dares contest the decisions he makes in the privacy of his tent, in the presence of all the parents. But Maïouf lived in Raqqa, the big city, and things worked differently there: you had to appear before a state judge, and the stepmother would have absolutely no influence over him.

A hearing was set up before the judge. Maïouf arrived alone; his mother was dead and there was no requirement for his father to be there, which was a relief. The young woman, though, came with her father. The judge attending to the case was a jowly man who couldn't have been less interested in Bedouin affairs.

He received them in his office and didn't make any fuss about releasing the two young people from their promise. Maïouf emerged, struggling to disguise his pride.

He'd won! He was free and, by the same token, he was no longer trapped by his stepmother's scheming. After what had just happened, now he'd inflicted this retraction on her, she wouldn't risk trying to impose her will on him again. There was still an enigma, though, a concern that sometimes stirred in Maïouf's heart of hearts: his father, the fact that his father had been oddly absent throughout these proceedings. Was the woman's power so all-encompassing, Maïouf wondered, that she not only had managed to supplant his mother, to reduce her to nothing, but also could arrogantly decide other people's fates to suit her jealous whims? She made all the decisions, that much was sure, and the power she exerted over Maïouf's father meant she could have whatever she wanted.

14

Maïouf, who was used to the rigors of desert life, didn't need much. Hardened by his years at school, he'd learned to tolerate the other pupils' jeers, which luckily grew rarer as he achieved increasingly good results. That didn't stop him from feeling sensitive about his poverty. Ever since he arrived he'd been wearing the same old djellaba. He wasn't the only one to dress like this, but more and more of his classmates wore European clothes. In fact, his old djellaba now betrayed his origins a little more blatantly every day.

It was a clear morning, the heat wasn't yet oppressive, and he had schoolwork to do—nothing unusual. But while he was sitting down at the small table that served as his desk a strange noise stopped him halfway. Defeated by the years of wear, his djellaba had just torn across the hip. He reached down for the strip of loose fabric, examined the tear, and soon realized it would be impossible to mend. He wasn't surprised. Truth be told, he'd been dreading this moment for a long time. He knew it would come eventually despite his precautions. It was hardly the time to make a fuss. He didn't have a choice: he'd have to change his clothes. The family who put a roof over his head had already given him so much; it wouldn't be appropriate to ask them for a new djellaba. But neither could he go to school in this drab, threadbare thing fraying in every direction and now literally falling to pieces. Changing clothes without borrowing . . . What choice did he have but to *buy*?

It was market day. Maïouf knew that his father would be coming to Raqqa, and he decided to go and find him. He was his father but, more important, he was the only person Maïouf could ask for money. The bottom line was that a djellaba wouldn't be a huge expense to him. Of course there'd been the business with the marriage which Maïouf had contested in his own way and caused to fail—and this amounted to an offense of sorts. But his father hadn't said anything. Maybe he didn't care about all that. Maybe his father's feelings toward him weren't actually contempt or loathing so much as indifference.

Maïouf set off toward the large square where all the buying and selling in the city took place, a little anxious at the thought of seeing his father, yes, but strengthened in his resolve by the shred of wool fabric rubbing against him as he clamped it to his hip.

When he reached his destination, the place was already buzzing with activity and the sun high in the sky. He didn't waste any time, immediately scouring the noisy, brightly colored crowd for his father. He hoped he'd find him among the middlemen who handled auctions and sales. From a distance he couldn't see him, and had to press deep into the teeming masses.

He weaved through some panicking sheep being ineptly herded by children who were hardly more confident than their flock. He slipped between groups of men, through dust and shouts, then walked along a small esplanade where fat, smug, pot-bellied men—unquestionably tradesmen—sat stuffing their faces with sandwiches and swilling them down with arak and Coca-Cola just to show how well they were doing. They'll be drunk before the end of the day, Maïouf thought as he passed them. He climbed over bolts of cloth, then onto some badly made crates that threatened to collapse; he was scolded, pushed, and jostled but he didn't back down before finally spotting his father. He gave a hesitant wave.

If his father saw him, he showed no indication of it. He stayed sitting there in the armchair kept specially for him— because he was an important man—and eyed the crowd as if it belonged to him and him alone. It was mid-morning and the moment came when all the Bedouins had arrived to sell or trade their livestock so the auctioning could start. The man in charge of organizing this great event was in the center of the square, and Maïouf could see him gesticulating and shouting into the crush. His father, though, sat a little way back, watching the scene from his armchair. Of all the buyers he was the only one to be offered a chair, and standing behind him—bolt upright, motionless, and suitably respectful—were his sons.

The crowd was thinner in places and as Maïouf came closer he was convinced his father had seen him: to prove it, his half brothers were openly watching his approach. True, he was no longer a child shyly coming to visit his father; yes, he'd grown, but his father was a man of status. And, conscious that he was coming to ask him for something, Maïouf felt insignificant before this man he knew to be a powerful figure.

When he was very close, his father didn't so much as uncross his arms—and he kept them crossed for the whole exchange—but simply looked away. Maïouf was wearing his torn djellaba. There was a scornful flicker in his father's eye. Despite the wall of silence greeting him, Maïouf bravely explained his situation, his need, his urgent necessity. He concluded his halting words by asking for a little money to buy a new djellaba, then looked down and waited for a reply. His father's teeth stayed clenched. The silence continued, excruciatingly. Eventually, still without a word, his father stood up, turned on his heel, and walked right into the crowd, abandoning the humiliated boy behind him. Maïouf's half brothers followed him. Maïouf didn't see them, since he'd kept his head down, but he heard their sneering laughter and hated them for it.

Once alone, Maïouf cried—though he'd never admit it later. He cried with humiliation and rage. Well, if that was how it was he wouldn't have anything more to do with his family. They no longer existed for him. His only family was his mother, and she was dead. He was an orphan. He drove every connection from his heart, hardened it, made it as cold as this wounding reality. If that was how it was, he wouldn't ask. He would take.

He knew his father had credit in a particular shop in Raqqa. He went there full of determination and introduced himself as his father's son, then chose a djellaba and charged it to his

father's account. The shopkeeper hesitated for a moment: Maïouf
had no reference from his father. With his torn clothes he didn't
even look rich enough to be his son. But, despite his disheveled
appearance, Maïouf's attitude must have struck the man as suf-
ficiently dignified—unless he just took pity on him—because he
wrote the price of the djellaba at the bottom of a list of numbers
scribbled in a ledger. When Maïouf was back out on the street
he felt neither pride nor relief. He'd settled the score. But now,
he knew, he could never turn to his relatives again. And he
didn't care.

15

The sun lit up the horizon and as Maïouf reached the sinister whitish building he thought it looked almost cheerful. Several horses were tied up to pillars along one facade, and the entrance was filled with constant comings and goings. Some were coming to collect administrative papers, others picking up driving licenses or seeking planning permission to build a house, and there were employees arriving in nonchalant little groups.

Even the desert seemed busy this morning as it blasted the perimeter wall with eddies of sand driven down from the nearby hills. And when you stepped inside, sand crunched underfoot all the way up to the top floor. Raqqa's administrative building included the law courts. It had been built only three years earlier, in the days when Maïouf had his first taste of being in love. It was new but already looked very old, tired, and timeworn.

The doors swung mournfully in the wind—and those were the ones still on their hinges. Some had simply been removed and never replaced. The elevator no longer worked; perhaps it never had. There was no space set aside for leaving shoes before going up the stairs. People left them where they could, where they wanted, where they hoped they'd find them again on the way out.

When construction work had started on the building, it had been talked about all over the city. Maïouf had come to observe the site; he'd never seen anyone undertake to erect such a big building. He was soon captivated by the trucks, the noise, the dust, and the battle against the desert. And he'd often come back after school to see the progress, sometimes staying for hours watching bricklayers at work high up on the shaky wooden scaffolding on the fourth floor.

Occasionally, a paunchy man would appear at the site, wending his way between heaps of sand and wooden supports. At first Maïouf struggled to work out what this man was doing there; he seemed important, and was always trailed by assistants laden with rolls of paper which they unfurled, from time to time, doing lots of pointing. The man would inspect, comment, decide, give instructions to the laborers. But Maïouf got the feeling he was there for something else. He spent most of his time in discussions with high-ranking officials or signing papers handed to him by humble-looking people who'd been waiting to see him, all day in some cases. It was only much later that Maïouf realized he was an architect. The man most likely attracted his attention because, to his mind, he incarnated a fascinating kind of influence, the sort of influence whose impact he'd borne since his earliest childhood, and it was based on exercising power.

This image of the architect—who strolled about with no specific purpose and dispensed his instructions to the laborers clustering around him—this was somehow mingled with the image of his father, which in turn was associated with the image of his father's sons, some of whom had never been to school and refused to work but spent most of their time swanning about with their noses in the air and yelling at anyone who happened to be in their way.

Maïouf had grown up in pace with this building, counting up floors instead of years. As he entered young adulthood, he'd also started taking more of an interest in the life of this city he lived in. Beyond the construction site, Raqqa was a place where people from very varied backgrounds lived alongside each other, a place where social differences were felt more acutely than in the villages he'd known. Of course in those villages you came across powerful men, more powerful than others, like his father whom he now avoided thinking about, but relationships were established face-to-face, man-to-man, and were dictated by customs that everyone knew and respected. Here people were somehow anonymous. The bustling crowd in the market, the hurrying crowd on the avenues, the exhausted crowd of ordinary people, huge crowds everywhere. In all this to-and-fro, the only distinguishing feature of the powerful was how redundant they were. That was what Maïouf concluded from his observations. And he must have been partly right: by following this line of reason, he'd managed to grasp that the fat man on the building site was the architect.

As he headed toward the building now, Maïouf remembered being surprised he hadn't seen a single Palestinian involved in its construction. He'd looked for Palestinians, though, because their community had been hotly debated at the time. Their situation as a people in exile who had come and asked a sister nation for support, and the feeling that—through them—the entire Arab world was suffering failure and rejection on the international scene, had stirred up strong feelings for a while. In fact, as recently as the previous week he'd been involved in a heated debate about them.

Maïouf had latterly discovered the pleasure of impassioned conversation. And these conversations were all the more impassioned and bitter because he was still smarting deep inside from the last humiliation his father had subjected him to, a humiliation which had spawned an exacting instruction: never give in again. That was why, when a lively discussion started up among a group of pupils between lessons, he was always quick to launch into polemics and get carried away with the exaltation of his strong feelings. His passion and occasional vehemence had actually attracted the attention of the Muslim Brotherhood. They'd contacted him through one of his classmates, whose cousin was a member. The Muslim Brotherhood advocated a brand of Islamic fundamentalism which was starting to enjoy a degree of success among the very poorest section of the population, particularly because of the discrepancy in Syrian society between the official rhetoric of brotherliness and sharing, and a reality riddled with inequality and injustice.

Now, in those days Maïouf put justice before everything else. Ah, justice! Even before friendship or love. He was starting to grasp the miserable fate that Syrian society had in store for his Bedouin kinsmen. So he'd lent an ear to what the Brotherhood had to say. And he'd drawn new strength—founded on conviction—from their exhortations. With their arguments, they'd reinforced the resentment he felt toward powerful men like dignitaries or that architect. But not everything they claimed convinced him. He'd come to know a few young Jewish boys, and the concept that Judaism was evil incarnate seemed very strange to him. He'd also felt that the Brotherhood's interpretation of the Koran was unsophisticated. As for their condemnation of the Western world, he was too fond of the films from those faraway places to give that credence. He hadn't joined them, but had learned from them to view the world and certain customs around him with a critical eye.

16

Once inside, Maïouf set off down a corridor that ran along the front of the building. The interior was no more attractive than the exterior. Chipped paintings that no one noticed anymore, the floor covered in a film of sand, none of the solemnity you might be entitled to expect in a place where justice was done. Maïouf didn't know which room he needed to go to, and he could only assume he had come to the right one when he saw the small groups of people talking animatedly beside an open door. He slowed when he reached the door and risked a quick glance into the small dusty room, from which he could hear a general hubbub punctuated by louder outbursts of talking. He wondered whether after all he was in the wrong place, but was told that this really was the courtroom, so he went in.

The first thing you noticed in the room was a portrait of the president hanging on the dingy wall. It looked as if it had been hung there in a hurry when someone noticed there wasn't one. The glass was covered in a thick layer of grime but he could still make out the faded colors and the same pose seen in all the presidential portraits in shops, on billboards, and in newspapers. Beyond a shadow of a doubt, this was the Father of the Nation, watching over its administration even in this small courtroom in this small city.

There was a great crowd of people inside, filling the space and constantly in motion. Maïouf managed to see that two tables had been set up at a slight angle to each other, under the portrait. Between the shoulders of densely packed, inquisitive onlookers, he could just see a fat man dripping with sweat who mopped his brow with a handkerchief from time to time and then, turning with some difficulty, put the hankie back in his trousers pocket. While his right hand carried out this little performance, his left hand flitted through the air, displaying his impatience with the other people—all as fat and sweaty as he was—who kept gathering around him. Before trying to find somewhere better to stand, Maïouf noticed one last detail: one of the men wore a shapeless hat that tipped down toward the nape of his neck.

In the end Maïouf decided to tuck himself in beside the doorway. From there he could watch the proceedings unnoticed. He was keen not to be seen, and this was easier for him today because for once he fitted in. His keffiyeh and djellaba didn't do anything to distinguish him from dozens of other people around him wearing the same things. None of them looked very interested in the case being tried, but that didn't matter to Maïouf: this wasn't the case he'd come to watch.

All at once there was shouting and a flurry of activity from the area where the president posed, unperturbed, in his frame.

The crowd surged forward with a combination of curiosity and strange satisfaction. Most of the people there had been drawn by the scandal of the case. Maïouf stood on tiptoe. Behind the second table now stood a man with his wrists in handcuffs, chained to two police officers. The sudden commotion was because this man had leapt to his feet and raised his arms, dragging the chains and the men attached to them along with him. In this comic tableau—the three men with their arms in the air shouting across each other—the accused was shouting the loudest.

"Let me go and find a liar!" he bellowed. "I can't have this one talking on his own. Let me go and find my own liar! I promise I'll come back."

He gesticulated wildly, still accompanied by the two police officers, who couldn't help joining in, and he turned his distraught, reddened face toward the man in the shapeless hat.

Maïouf leaned close to the man beside him.

"What's going on?" he asked.

"A Bedouin shepherd. He killed a man who wanted his sheep. He says the whole village agreed he could kill him, they'd had a meeting about it and even the victim's family thought it fair. He told the judge the *mukhtar* had endorsed the decision."

The man puffed himself up self-importantly as he gave this account, hardly looking at Maïouf while he talked. He seemed to be enjoying the scandal, and was already savoring the fact that, over the next few days, he could describe this to anyone who cared to listen.

"These wretched Bedouins!" he added. "This one's been getting angry, saying people in Raqqa should mind their own business and leave the Bedouins alone. He says that where he comes from if you kill someone and don't apologize you'll be executed anyway, or 'have an accident.' You should have seen the judge's face when he said that!"

With this, the man launched into a long loud laugh. Maïouf would have been happy to leave it at that but the man was on a roll.

"And then," he said with laughter still in his voice, "this is the best bit: he said that, in his village, if you kill someone by accident or by mistake you still have to pay! But that if the village agrees to it, well, then justice has been done."

Maïouf was familiar with these customs. They may have been primitive, but they had their own logic. All Bedouins respected them, and these laws governed their lives just as well as any others might. What could this man from Raqqa understand about that when he so obviously despised the Bedouin? Maïouf kept his thoughts to himself but didn't want to appear rude by ignoring the man.

"Why does he want to find a liar?" he asked.

"Because he doesn't know what an attorney is. Look, can you see the man in the hat over there, facing him? He's the public prosecutor. He's just finished his speech for the prosecution. The Bedouin is challenging it. He thinks he's at a lying competition and he's asking to be allowed to choose his own champion."

The judge had leaned against the back of his chair and was mopping his brow with mounting irritation. He suddenly sat up with unexpected energy and called for silence. People took barely any notice, carrying on with their muttering, but a little more quietly. Exhausted by the effort and by the indifference of the crowd, the judge slumped back into his chair. But he wouldn't admit defeat.

"That's enough now!" He bellowed authoritatively. Then he turned to the accused and asked, "You want to make a fuss? I'll give you what you deserve." Now he looked over at the public prosecutor, who'd been left speechless by the outburst, and added, "There's no point continuing. We're both wasting our time. I've decided what needs to be done with this one."

The prosecutor waved a hand to mean he accepted the judge's decision, and returned to his seat. His relief at not having to make any further contribution was clear to see.

Maïouf didn't listen as the judge handed down a hefty sentence to the stunned defendant, who didn't understand what was going on at all. He hardly even noticed the judge leaving through a side door, or the trouble the policemen had getting the Bedouin back to his feet. The terror that had been gnawing at him since he entered the courtroom was now so acute his ears were ringing. What hope was there for his young uncle, who was also a Bedouin, with a judge like this?

His poor uncle!

One of the few smiling faces that greeted him when he went back to the village. His young uncle who'd never had his luck, nor perhaps his ordeals to strengthen his will. After only a few years he'd had to stop his schooling. But because he'd spent some time at a desk he hadn't had the tough apprenticeship as a shepherd so they'd had to find a different job for him. On the other hand, he could read and write, and that had helped him. He'd joined the police force.

That was how, back in the spring, he'd ended up in an isolated guardroom on a road through the desert. It was a block of cement which got hot enough to cook a man, and had two iron beds, one for the police officer and one for him, and a collection of rusty cooking utensils. All he had to do there was wait. Just wait.

One morning the uncle had turned up in the village wild-eyed and covered in blood. The police officer was dead. There'd been an accident. He'd been cleaning his rifle when the shot fired. The body had fallen onto the gray dust of the floor. He'd turned it over, but it was too late. He'd been terrified, had grabbed the rifle without even thinking, and fled. Oh, if only he'd stayed there; if only he'd called the telephone exchange; if only he hadn't tried to help the police officer, who was covered in blood; if only he hadn't picked up the rifle. If only . . .

The police had swarmed into the village toward the end of the day. They'd had no trouble finding Maïouf's uncle, who was hiding in his mother's house, and they'd marched him away. He was now accused of murder.

17

Several months earlier Maïouf had decided to visit his grand-mother, see his father's village, and, if he felt he had the strength, go to the house itself. His resentment toward his family had ended up weighing heavily on him, and perhaps because they didn't know what had caused this rancor, his relatives couldn't understand it. Why had he stopped sending news? When he arrived shortly after sunrise the street was unusually busy. People had greeted him with obvious delight after such a long absence, but something that had happened the day before was on every mind and in every conversation.

They were all standing on doorsteps talking and gesticulating, clearly excited, particularly when someone who didn't know anything about the drama turned up. He heard at least fifteen different versions that day, and there would be more over the next few days. It became increasingly difficult to work out exactly what had happened.

Each member of the village embroidered the facts and invented new details, either to make the story more epic or to entertain him.

He hadn't really succeeded in getting to the bottom of it. He'd stayed there for a few days without managing to see his father and, saddened, he'd ended up driving every variation of the saga from his mind.

A few weeks after he'd returned to Raqqa he'd come across a sheep trader whose family all lived in the village. They'd chatted about one thing and another, the weather they were having now and the weather to come, and passed on news of their acquaintances.

The old trader had tried hard enough to avoid mentioning the incident, but it was impossible for either of them to pretend it hadn't happened.

"You know, I'm a Badawi myself, but I couldn't do anything to help, believe me. They looked absolutely determined and we were out of our depth, we didn't even know what to accuse them of!"

Seeing that Maïouf was impatient to hear more, he continued with resignation in his voice as he said, "Oh, you'll criticize me too . . . But, well, like I said, those men had definitely been in the area a long time. Everyone thinks they were there even before dawn because the dogs had barked at the desert that night.

"I had some ewes due to give birth at the time so I got up a bit earlier than usual, you know it's best to keep an eye on them then: you never know what might happen, and one ewe lost is a promise of hardship. You know, only last week I had to go and get one from the very middle of . . . All right, don't get so worked up, I'll go right back to the beginning for you, well, not the very beginning, I'll tell you about that if you like, but from the morning itself, from when we saw your uncle turn up covered in blood. Like I said, they hadn't shown their faces yet, they came later. But to get back to your uncle, we heard the police car coming from a long way off. Everyone knew that's what it was because apart from your father's truck, there aren't many vehicles in the area, and you end up recognizing the tone of every engine. D'you know, it's not that long since they actually gave cars to the police. But, well, it's helpful for us, even when we don't have anything to feel guilty about!

"All those years we got used to seeing them turn up on horseback unannounced and creeping up on us in the middle of fields or the village so it's quite a relief knowing they're in a car. At least we can hear them coming now.

"The police don't usually come around so early. You know what they're like, they don't have much to do and they're not very bright. You know I won't say a bad word about your uncle but, all the same, he's no genius! When they should get off their backsides it's always something too important for them to deal with, and their superiors send someone else to take care of it. Anyway, people would rather not see them. No disrespect, but you know they act like they own the place and when they need money, they just have to put the pressure on. Anyone who refuses, even if he hasn't committed a crime, can't help being in the wrong and will soon find he's in all sorts of trouble. So they have a nice life in their little guardroom and they stir themselves only when it's time to eat. They have a bit of a drive around in the mornings to use up the regulation amount of fuel, and another one in the afternoon after prayers when the heat's dropped a bit. But no one can remember ever seeing or hearing them doing anything strenuous or getting up in the night. Quite the opposite, really, there are times when they don't even leave their guardroom for a day or two because they're so exhausted from doing nothing. Anyway, because there are only two of them, they don't have much cause to go to any trouble. Which is why the sound of that engine when it was still dark woke quite a few people. Some got up and went out to see what was going on. The car came hurtling into the village and stopped right in the middle, in a cloud of dust and feathers. Because it had also woken all the chickens, they came squawking from every direction and ran toward the headlights. Given how your uncle was driving, he must have crushed a fair few. Luckily, as you know, my cousin's house is at the other end of the village and the chickens he keeps for me weren't harmed. Because with the price you pay for them at the moment, I don't know how I'd have managed to buy more. Nowadays you can't even buy one for the price you'd have paid for two last year. D'you know, only earlier today I was trying to buy . . . Stop yelling the whole time: if you keep interrupting me, we'll never get there! I'll tell you everything, but I do have to tell you how it was, and if I don't give you all the details, you might not understand . . . So the police car stopped and your uncle got out straightaway. We were surprised because he's not usually the one driving, he's too young. He was pale, but what we noticed first was the blood, fresh blood all over the front of his uniform. The people who'd come outside went over to him and started asking questions. There was such a racket you couldn't hear a word. Men asked him what was going on, whether there was a war, women screamed. Eventually, one of the women shrieked louder than the others, saying he might be injured and they should see if he needed help. That calmed everyone down and he could talk then. He wasn't injured, but he said he'd killed his colleague."

18

"Please don't interrupt me, if you stop me every time I open my mouth, I'll miss the market and you won't find out what you want to know. I said I'd give you all the details. At the time no one made the connection between what was happening to your uncle and the men they'd heard. He wasn't even the one to mention them first. And, actually, afterward I thought it was really strange he hadn't said anything about them when they were the only bit of news we'd had in the area for a long time. If you want my opinion, I'm sure there's something not right about this whole business. But let me get on with it, otherwise I'll lose the thread again and we'll never get it over with. Your uncle sat down on the running board of the car and started to cry. Everyone gathered around him in a circle, and no one was talking now. Then he calmed down and started telling his story:

"'For a few days now,' he said, 'my colleague and I have been on edge but we didn't really know why. Maybe it was the onset of spring that was getting to us, because those days and nights without a woman stuck in the middle of the desert, in that block of cement where the heat can cook you alive, with the same old iron beds, the same old pots and pans, the same teapot that's been rusting for years, it ends up getting you down. So we decided to go out for a drive to calm our nerves.'"

The sheep trader paused, knowing how to create an effect.

"That was when someone started asking him about the strangers, but he didn't like that at all. 'There's no need to talk about them,' he almost screamed; 'it's nothing to do with them! I can tell you want me to talk about them, but there's no way I'm going to. Nothing to do with it, I tell you, nothing to do with it!' No one said anything because you know it's best not to contradict policemen, even if you know them well. Otherwise it won't be long before they turn up on your doorstep with sweet smiles on their faces. They chat about one thing and another and, while they're at it, they mention that they don't earn much and they'd be very happy if you gave them a chicken, a sheep, or even some money. If it was their birthday every time we had to give them a present, they'd be a couple of thousand years old by now! But your uncle was getting so wound up and we couldn't seem to calm him. So someone asked why he said he'd killed his colleague and why he was covered in blood. He started crying again and it was quite a while before he could talk.

"Eventually he said, 'We did a few rounds yesterday to check, because those men were there and that's not normal. But there's not much point in my telling you about that because it has nothing to do with this.' He clammed up, went silent for a while, then went on: 'We just checked, that's all, and there was nothing going on, absolutely nothing. We'd driven far out into the desert for nothing, not even a crow in sight. But because of all that we couldn't sleep. Mind you, we were also getting fed up with the place, we spend all day and all night there. Being on the main road doesn't help much, you get trucks and buses passing from time to time, but you end up getting to know them all and they don't even wake us now. Except this time we just couldn't get to sleep, with all this business.'

"At that point, someone asked, 'But what business?' seeing as he kept saying nothing was going on. He started crying again, and couldn't stop. I had to give him a good shake to get him to go on with his story.

"He said, 'Our guardroom's isolated and if anything happened to us, there wouldn't be much point in calling the main station because it would take them at least two hours to get here. So we decided that if we were ever in any danger, we needed to know how to defend ourselves without any help. OK, so nothing's actually happened since I started the job, but you never know. And because nothing's happened and we haven't had to use our rifles or pistols for a long time, we thought we should clean them and check they were working in case we needed them. We started to disassemble to oil all the parts. Good we thought of it because there was sand in the cylinders and they wouldn't have worked when we needed them. Not that we needed them then, that's not what I meant, but that's when the accident happened . . . He was putting his pistol back together and I'd finished mine. So I said I was going to try firing it outside because it was a cloudless night and you could see well by moonlight. We put some old tins along the wall facing the door to the guardroom to practice. I backed away to take a shot at the tins and make sure my pistol was working properly. I didn't look at the door while I was taking aim, and just as I fired he came out of the guardroom and walked past the tins. I yelled at him but it was already too late and he fell straight to the ground. At the time I thought he was mucking about and I shouted at him to stop it, it wasn't funny. But he stayed there, not moving, so I ran over, still yelling at him. I crouched down and rolled him over, and his eyes were just staring into space . . .'

"Your uncle stopped talking, his throat was so tight he couldn't say any more. We got him to drink some tea and asked him to keep going. He stopped crying and got angry with us. 'I've told you everything,' he said. 'Leave me alone!' We asked why he'd come to the village instead of calling the station and he said he was frightened, he said, 'To be honest, I didn't think, I jumped in the car and drove to the village to ask for your help in case anyone came to give me grief.'"

The old trader broke off, trying to avoid Maïouf's eyes.

"So that's what happened," he said. "Now I'd better get to the market . . ."

"I know you well enough to know we could go on chatting for hours and you wouldn't think once about your sheep. You know it's the next bit I'm really interested in."

"We were all standing around him," the old man went on in a glum voice, "and no one missed a single word but now that he'd stopped there was this long silence. And that's when we heard a car engine getting closer. I was watching your uncle, and he got to his feet and came and stood among us. I could see he was shaking, but at the time I didn't think anything of it because I put it down to the emotion from what had happened. But later I remembered it was just when we heard an engine away in the distance, and the closer that sound got the more your uncle shook. By the time the jeep arrived at the end of the street he could hardly stand on his own two legs."

19

"A man got out of the jeep and asked what was going on. We didn't get a look at him because his keffiyeh was up over his face, but we all noticed a big scar across his right eye, it made him look strange, almost frozen, the eye looked as set as the scar. On top of that, he had this voice like nothing I've ever heard, not near the village, not in Raqqa, not even in Aleppo. The next day I even asked some of the others about it, but no one else knew that voice either. I'd recognize it anywhere because it was so odd, metallic sounding, with an accent I couldn't place. The hadjis think it's a Saudi accent, but they're not sure. There were two other men in the jeep. No one knows what they looked like because they didn't get out. Either way, it was unusual seeing them in the village because there's nothing to bring strangers to the place, the main road's quite a long way away and there's no sign to say the village is there. You lived in your grandmother's house long enough before moving away to know you have to know how to get here or really stumble across it by chance. When you're in the desert you can be a couple of hundred meters away and still not see it because of the dip in the land. So they must have come because they had a reason. The man said they were on a journey and had been on the road a long time. They'd stopped on the main road for a rest and heard gunshots. Almost immediately after that they saw the police car tearing past and they followed it. That's how they got to the village. There again, none of us thought that through at the time because so much had happened in the last hour that we'd have believed anything. But when we talked about it afterward, no one had ever heard of anyone who chased after police cars in the middle of the night without a good reason. The man really wanted to know what had happened, he wouldn't give up. Normally, no one would say anything but given the circumstances, plenty of people felt like talking because, with all the goings-on, we'd have weeks' worth of gossip in the village. You know what it's like: the more you do to create memories, the better it is afterward . . . He was a funny sort: he looked almost happy when we said your uncle had just killed his colleague. While all this was going on, your uncle hadn't said a word, but now I come to think of it, I'm convinced he was frightened. It wasn't normal for him to go on shaking like that. When he saw the guy smiling he seemed relieved. But he started shaking again when the man came over and muttered something in his ear. No one heard what he said, but your uncle nodded. He got into the car with them and they left."

"And you let him go?"

The trader looked up, surprised.

"Well, they hadn't done anything wrong."

"Just now you said they looked very determined, and now you're saying there were three of them against the whole village . . ." Maïouf protested.

"Your uncle didn't make a fuss, I swear it, it was almost like he knew them. He was frightened, but he followed them without a word and didn't seem to want anything from us. He even left the police car right where it was and made it clear to everyone he was OK with these men."

"The Bedouin don't usually let strangers bundle one of their kind into a car, that's all," Maïouf muttered. "When someone takes refuge with the Bedouin, he's safe, you know that. You know better than I do that our people would rather be killed than hand over someone who's put trust in them, whatever the reason."

"You're a bit too full of yourself, young man," the trader replied curtly. "You're happy to judge everyone because you've done all that studying. You haven't taken your baccalauréat yet and you're acting like some sort of professor already! It's easy to talk like that. You know, I'm one of the last who still remembers the big flocks, when the whole tribe, masses of us, drove hundreds of camels and thousands of sheep. When we came to a stop in the middle of the desert, we'd put up all our tents and it was like a whole town suddenly being born as the sun went down and the shooting stars came out. And then people started saying we couldn't go here and couldn't go there, we had to start taking a census, registering with the local authorities, we weren't allowed to trade . . . In the early days we managed to put up a fight, we hid our children when the census officials came around so they couldn't be registered and drafted into the army, or if they questioned the numbers we'd show them different children who were bigger or older. But it didn't help much . . . We were driven out, penned into specific areas. It's only recently that we've stayed in the village all year . . . Do you think this country likes us? You'll see when you grow up, you'll see how people watch you, how they treat you. And you'll also realize the more you fight, the more you rebel, the more they'll pursue you, the more they'll drive you down, the more they'll break you. That's why I always look twice now before sticking my neck out. You have to understand your uncle wasn't putting up any resistance. Everyone thought he was lying, he wasn't trusting us with the truth. And given he'd just said he'd killed his colleague, even if it was by mistake, no one really felt like standing up for him. But he wasn't in any danger or, at least, he didn't say he was: when the man said they were taking him to Raqqa, he got into the jeep without a word. And that's the truth."

"I'm sorry," Maïouf said, looking away. "I didn't mean to insult you. But I'm sad because I now know too much about this, and I wish it could be different."

"Maybe that's because you're young," the old man said. "As for me, I'm off to sell my sheep."

And he walked away wearily, his back stooped.

20

Once the first case had been concluded the crowd grew restless.

Chairs were vacated, and there was a lot of coming and going. New people arrived and looked for a seat to watch the next case: that of Maïouf's uncle. The latest events were being discussed on all sides. Maïouf was shoved aside several times. He clearly couldn't stay where he was without being trampled underfoot. He didn't want to get lost in the crowd of gawking sensation-seekers, so he stepped outside to get some fresh air until the hearings started again.

As he walked out through the imposing front doorway, Maïouf was dazzled by the harsh morning light reflecting off the sand as if off a flat sea. The big steps were the scene of constant to-ing and fro-ing, which meant he couldn't sit down. He walked around the building, and found that the northern side was quieter and afforded a few welcome areas of shade.

Maïouf chose one and crouched down to calm his nerves. He thought he'd stay there a matter of minutes but succumbed to a long daydream.

He remembered the moment when, with his heart hammering, he'd dared to speak to the young girl living next door. He'd been introduced to her not long before by the daughter of the house where he lived. But the introductions had been rushed, halfhearted. He'd been on his way out when they met. She hadn't really seemed to notice him but he was very taken with her. And he'd been obsessed by her ever since. Which is why on his way home from school on this particular day he'd dragged his heels so he'd be outside her house just as she arrived home. He'd watched her so often that he had an accurate idea of her timetable, and knew exactly when he'd see her. When she appeared, he quickened his pace to be in step with her.

"Good evening!" he ventured.

She looked at him with a pretense of surprise and some amusement.

"I don't think I know you," she replied with mock severity. "Do you think a girl should speak to a stranger in the street? And if she does, would you have any respect for her?"

As she said this, the girl's face broke into a smile, a slight flush of red still stealing over her cheeks from when he'd spoken to her.

"But we do know each other!" he protested. "Don't you remember?"

The girl shook her head: no. A little disappointed to be so easily forgotten, Maïouf decided to change his tactics.

"We come across each other often, you know. I live next door to you."

"What a coincidence!"

Her laugh was so clear, so spontaneous that he was won over by her cheerfulness and—partly out of happiness, partly out of relief—burst out laughing himself. They walked together like this for a while, laughing but embarrassed. Secretly, he was ecstatic. A boundless pleasure was filling his lungs and accelerating his heart rate. She'd agreed to talk to him! She even seemed happy! A dream was shaping up as reality. He couldn't believe it was possible. Luckily, it wasn't he himself talking and laughing—oh no! It was someone else with his face, and he was watching him do it, admiring his composure.

All the same, he was worried that a long silence might ruin this first exchange, and was on the point of launching into a long description of something when she interrupted him with a charming tilt of her head.

"Well, I hope we'll see each other again."

And she'd turned away and walked through her door without another word. He stayed there on the sidewalk, sorry he couldn't talk to her any longer but intoxicated because he hadn't been rejected. He'd sung to himself all evening and, for the first time ever, didn't throw himself into his books after the evening meal.

The following day they'd met again, and the day after that, and every day since. But Fadia—that was her name, a name he said over and over with a sense of wonderment—hadn't agreed to meet him except for these engineered "chance" encounters on the way home from school. So at the end of every afternoon he rushed out into the street and waited for her to appear. She'd guessed what he was up to but had accepted it with a graciousness full of promise.

He even got the feeling she enjoyed their conversations, which often went on for some time outside her front door. This must be it, the ideal love that Sufis talked about. Taking pleasure in someone else's company. Sharing her happiness and deep-seated hopes, being luminously in communion with her. The very act of imagining Fadia's body, of being drawn into erotic fantasies about her, seemed degrading in comparison with these noble feelings. He could think of Fadia only in the words of the great poet Omar Khayyam, whose vision of happiness was "water, grass, and the contemplation of a beautiful face."

Someone shouted farther up the street, startling Maïouf. The trial! He leapt to his feet, noticed that the sun had moved across the sky, and ran around to the main entrance of the building.

21

The prosecution speech was drawing to a close.

"So, your honor, this boy is claiming it was an accident. Who could ever prove that, when the only witness is no longer with us to corroborate it? I say that if his version were true we wouldn't have found his clothes covered in blood. If his version were true we wouldn't have found the crime weapon at his home. No, if it was an accident, he wouldn't have fled the scene. An accident . . . would have meant he had nothing to fear."

Pausing briefly to let his arguments sink in, the public prosecutor grasped his trousers, which had slipped down with the constant wobbling of his stomach, and jerked them back up, savoring the murmurs of onlookers.

"The accused fled, then," he went on. "But let's be clear about this. He didn't run just anywhere. He took refuge in his village, with his family, among the Bedouin who—as we saw earlier—are against our country's legal system, the Bedouin who think they can dispense justice themselves!"

Hearing these words, Maïouf felt as if scalding oil were being poured into his veins. Judging by the silence in the crowd, he wasn't alone in finding them insulting. Even the judge tried to temper the prosecutor's aggressive words. But reveling in his own theatrics, the prosecutor didn't notice; he was as unstoppable as a racehorse.

"You now know," he said, "that the Bedouin are cunning creatures, they'll do whatever it takes to be right."

The judge then sat forward slightly and raised his hand unambiguously at the man in the hat to get him to stop what could easily become dangerous provocation for a crowd which included a good many Bedouin.

Had the prosecuting lawyer described them as "cunning"? Maïouf smiled to himself, but it was a bitter smile. Yes, the Bedouin were cunning, but had they been given any choice? Without their cunning, how could they have survived the pitfalls of the desert? This cunning, inculcated in them by a hostile natural world, had served them many a time against their enemies, and they had it to thank for avoiding pointless bloodshed. Yes, the Bedouin were cunning. But could you say that his young uncle had behaved cunningly when he ran away? It was laughable to scramble things up like that.

While Maïouf chewed over his own bitterness, the prosecutor carried on with his performance, raising his voice to give the final movement more operatic impact.

"What was the accused hoping to find in his village? The answer to that is clear: he was hoping for protection. But what protection does an innocent man need? And, more important, is he innocent?" Another pause, shorter this time, then he raised his arms to the heavens as he said, "Answer these questions, your honor, and your judgment will be made. His flight, the weapon, the blood—everything incriminates this boy. And the dead man's blood splattered over his clothes demands justice!"

Now that he'd finished, he let his arms drop. A peculiarly dense silence weighed on the room for a moment, then tumult broke out. Half the audience cheered the speech while the other half were on their feet shouting insults at the prosecutor. The tension was electrifying: people were turning on each other; some left the room, throwing their arms in the air vehemently. Maïouf took the opportunity to spot a few people he knew. He saw acquaintances from the village dotted here and there, but neither his grandmother nor his aunt. In the end he turned all his attention on his uncle.

The young man had all but collapsed, with his hands crossed on the table, flanked by those of the policemen he was chained to. He looked overwhelmed, his face alarmingly pale. For all the world like a guilty man cornered. Maïouf felt fear flood through him again. The thought of Fadia's smile had driven it away for a while, but the sight of his only friend so powerless revived it. What could he do? He moved away from the wall to attract the attention of his uncle, whose blank gaze roved over the crowd without ever settling. When his eyes met Maïouf's they locked onto them and filled with avid hope, like those of an exhausted animal stumbling across water after a sandstorm. But that hope was painful to Maïouf. He noticed his uncle straighten his shoulders and find the strength to manage a tired smile. Filled with despair, Maïouf leaned back against the wall.

The judge had withdrawn to deliberate. It seemed to go on forever and Maïouf couldn't bear the tension so he decided to step out of the room, but not outside this time. He went into the relative cool of the corridor and started pacing up and down.

When the judge came back in, all the people wandering in the corridor returned to their places and Maïouf went back into the hearing room. Grumbling to himself, the judge sat down and invited the lawyers to do so too. The accused was ashen, his mouth gaping open indecently as he stared at the man on whom his future depended. He was half standing from his chair, as if anticipating a cataclysm. Maïouf was full of dread.

The judge spoke at last:

"You have said what you had to say. Now I shall decide the sentence: the accused is found guilty. He is condemned to twenty years' imprisonment."

Maïouf felt as if his throat had been crushed. He could feel tears welling in his eyes. He ran outside, into the corridor, the entrance hall, to the bottom of the steps of this building that once so fascinated him but now filled him with shame. It took him a long time to control his emotions, longer even than he thought it had because when he became aware of his surroundings again, he found he was in a throng of people who'd watched his uncle's trial and were now leaving. One came so close Maïouf could hear what he was saying.

"The judge went too far. He knows the poor kid doesn't have the money to pay the police to plead in his favor."

Without thinking, Maïouf snatched at the man's sleeve.

"Do you mean the trial could have been rigged with false witnesses? Is that possible?"

The man roared with sneering laughter, eyeing Maïouf's djellaba.

"You're obviously a Bedouin," he said. "I bet you don't come to the city much. And, yes, of course trials can be rigged, and sometimes the judge is even greedier than the police! You just need to have the money . . ."

22

What really happened that night Maïouf learned from his young uncle himself. He'd made Maïouf swear never to talk about it; both their lives depended on that.

One evening, the future victim had been surprised to hear noises on the far side of the sand dune: a horse whinnying and the sound of a car engine being cut. In that particular spot, the hills hug close together, creating a series of dips and hiding places. The man climbed up the dune but before reaching the summit, dropped cautiously to the ground and crawled to the crest.

Below him, two armed men were holding a terrified horse by the bridle. The policeman recognized the man riding the horse: he was one of the group fighting for the Bedouins' nomadic rights to these lands which they'd been traveling for millennia but from which they were now being driven out. He was a willful man, someone people listened to, and was starting to attract support from anyone who didn't want to be rammed into concrete tower blocks on the outskirts of cities. A third man, whose face was ravaged by a long scar over his right eye, came over to the group and brutally knocked the horseman from his mount. With the rider sprawled on the ground, the man coolly took aim with a pistol and shot him. The policeman, who had flattened himself against the dune to watch the scene, jumped to his feet and ran back to the guardroom.

Gasping for breath, he was just reaching the bunker when a jeep caught up with him, tracking him with its headlights. The man with the scar came over to Maïouf's young uncle and took his pistol from its holster. Then he turned to the other policeman, told him to kneel, and shot him at point-blank range. His blood spurted out, drenching his uniform. Maïouf's uncle thought he would suffer the same fate and threw himself to the floor, begging for mercy. The three men laughed, making fun of him and saying, "That's what'll happen to you if you tell anyone what we get up to in the desert, and if you don't tell everyone it was you who killed your colleague." Then they climbed back into the jeep and vanished into the night, leaving the young policeman on the point of collapse.

Maïouf's uncle found it difficult to relate these events, and didn't dare look his childhood friend in the eye. He managed only to beg him once again to keep the story completely secret.

Maïouf gave his word. But he swore to himself that he'd come back one day and try to do something for his people.

23

The circular had been hung on the wall at the National Ministry for Education and in regional offices in major cities, but no pupils had been contacted personally. Maïouf, who was constantly haunted by thoughts of his young uncle, had paid less attention than anyone else to the notice board. He'd worked his way through the three days of school-leaving exams with the same application he'd shown all these years, but he hadn't succeeded in feeling the least pride when he read in the paper a few days later that he'd achieved the highest score in the region in his baccalauréat.

Only Fadia gave him any comfort. Their relationship had evolved since they'd first met outside his lodgings. They saw each other frequently and strolled through the streets after he came home from school in the evening or whenever there was a public holiday. They went for little shopping trips together in the bazaar, spending hours gazing at stalls and imagining what they might buy if and when they earned some money. They also met in a park and would sit chatting in the shade of a tree; Maïouf did most of the talking, describing the deserts of his childhood. And, without his realizing it, Fadia had gradually come to fill his entire horizon. She'd become the center of his world, so that a day spent without her felt strangely empty.

It was actually Fadia who told him the news one evening.

"Why didn't you tell me you were going to Damascus?" she asked a little reproachfully.

He looked so surprised that she couldn't help laughing.

"Don't you know? You did come top in the whole region, didn't you?"

"Yes," he replied, still not understanding.

"Apparently, the top candidates from each region in the country have been invited to Damascus by the minister."

"You're just making fun of me!"

Maïouf had no intention of being hurtful when he said this; he simply couldn't believe it was true. Damascus had always seemed so inaccessible, and to find he'd been invited there by a minister—Maïouf, the little Badawi boy from the desert—was genuinely unimaginable. But sadness passed like a shadow over Fadia's face, and her eyes, which were always so bright, seemed to darken. When Maïouf noticed this he regretted being so abrupt and was quick to pick up the conversation again.

"And when's this meant to be happening?"

"In a couple of weeks, if I've got it right."

Damascus! Maïouf said to himself. What could the minister possibly want? Probably an official reception, handing out certificates, something like that. And would he have to make a speech? That prospect was more terrifying to Maïouf than anything else. He had little inclination to go bowing and scraping to dignitaries. Still, he'd never been to Damascus, and would he have another opportunity to go there, a Bedouin like him? He wasn't even sure he'd get beyond Raqqa. He might well have plans to apply to the university in Aleppo but it had to be said he'd never even seen the place except in photos. So Damascus!

Fadia's hand felt cool when it reached for his on the way to the bus. Maïouf had done some research: there would be twelve of them at the reception, representing the twelve regions of Syria. As for the education minister, he was a military man whose portrait Maïouf had once glimpsed but not really looked at. He had little hope of recognizing the minister.

It was a long journey. Maïouf had promised himself he'd enjoy the views, he wouldn't miss any of it, but the heat, the droning engine, the swaying and lurching all got the better of him and he fell asleep. Having left Raqqa in mid-afternoon, they traveled all night, stopping only for short breaks to fill up with fuel and give the passengers a chance to stretch their legs or drink a cup of scalding tea.

When Maïouf woke, dawn was just breaking. The bus was on a wide two-lane road which was already full of traffic. By the spreading flush of daylight, Maïouf saw nothing but huge construction sites between dirty-looking buildings and tightly packed rows of drab low-slung houses all the way up the steep hillside overlooking the city. Despite the opaque sunshade and stripes of color decorating the front windshield, he could see through it to a gloomy cloud hanging over the city and swallowing more and more of the horizon as the bus drove down from the heights toward Damascus.

24

As they drove through the suburbs Maïouf was filled with disappointment. Could this really be the capital, the site of the legendary Saladin's tomb? Everything looked gray in the dirty daylight, even the clusters of trees planted along the road. The huge Umayyad Mosque with its tall minarets and its cupola slowly flushing pink in the light of the rising sun failed to save him from disillusionment. Tired, stiff, and thirsty, he watched buildings spool past. The traffic grew heavier as they approached the city center, the sidewalks overflowed with people, and he caught himself missing the desert.

The bus came to a stop at last. Maïouf glanced at the clock in the bus station and realized he had an hour to get to the ministry. He made the most of the time to have a good look at the people in the streets. What struck him most in this unfamiliar city were the women. Many of them weren't wearing scarves, and none had any qualms about talking to strangers. He saw some walking together in groups, joshing and chatting or laughing loudly. Their clothes bordered on indecent: they wore their blouses almost unbuttoned, short skirts, and high heels. He thought of Fadia, her reserve and propriety, and the private, shaded little street where they met.

When he arrived at the ministry he was shown to a room where the other star candidates were already waiting. All ten boys were wearing trousers and jackets, and the only girl was also in European clothes. Maïouf was the only one in a djellaba. As he walked into the room, the man who'd shown him the way said, "With your clothes and your accent, there's no disguising you're a Bedouin." Then in a tart, humorless voice he added, "I hope you didn't dress like that to be provocative."

The waiting went on forever, and Maïouf silently tolerated the mocking comments being made behind his back. Eventually someone came to fetch them, and they were taken through a labyrinth of corridors and up several flights of stairs. Maïouf was so disoriented he wasn't sure he was still in the same building. The little group finally arrived in a room bathed in light by large bay windows which had been left open. Along one side of the room stood a long table covered in a white cloth and brightened at regular intervals with vases of flowers. Maïouf had never seen anything like them in his life. Nodding golden corollas alongside stems edged with tiny blue petals, and a cluster of white stars topped with bright scarlet foliage. But what really struck him were the large jugs of clear water, gleaming like precious jewels, like something straight out of folklore.

* * *

As a man of the desert, he was completely lost in contemplation of those jugs of water when a wailing siren right outside startled him. Men armed with submachine guns poured into the room and stood on either side of the large doorway at the far end. This was followed by an icy silence. Out in the corridor a door slammed, and guttural voices barked orders: the officials were on their way. Maïouf froze in spite of himself.

The minister came through the doorway. He was short and chubby, wearing a light-colored suit and heavy dark glasses that made him look like someone on a cruise. There was nothing military about him. Just behind him, two taller men also in dark glasses scanned the room with eagle-eyed intensity. Behind these three men were about a dozen photographers who probably followed the minister's every move and were constantly snapping shots of him. Before stepping onto the small stage that had been provided, the minister asked to be introduced to the graduates in person. He shook each of them by the hand and Maïouf felt that official hand glide into his. The minister finished his round by shaking the girl's hand, perhaps at rather greater length. Then he climbed the two steps to the stage and launched into a long speech, a very long speech.

This was an electioneering speech directed far more at the press than at the young students—even though they made an effort to be attentive—and the minister covered geopolitics, relations between Syria and other countries, the country's future, and the hope that Syria put in its young people and the intelligence of its future executives. When the minister had finished talking there was some applause and a crackle of camera flashes before everyone was invited to enjoy the buffet.

No one paid any attention to Maïouf but he dared not eat, despite being hungry. Or rather, eating was the last thing on his mind in the present circumstances. As for the journalists and photographers, who showed very little interest in the brilliant graduates, they'd thrown themselves on the food, not leaving much room for the bashful students. Crippled by his own embarrassment, Maïouf was trying to find the most unobtrusive place to stand when a voice whispered in his ear.

"What would you do, my boy," it said, "if you were offered a grant to study abroad?"

The minister was standing next to him, looking him right in the eye.

"I'd like to go to Germany to study agronomy," Maïouf said, inventing this reply without even thinking.

The minister looked surprised.

"Why agronomy? Our country is well equipped in that field and it strikes me that's not the biggest problem in your region."

"It could be soon."

Seeing the minister's face darken, Maïouf wondered whether he'd been too glib. But he didn't have time to redeem himself; the minister had turned his attention to the girl, who seemed to fascinate him far more than Maïouf's future.

25

Maïouf had been back in Raqqa about ten days when an official letter arrived for him. He was being summoned to the Ministry of Education in Damascus in three days' time. There, he would be given a grant to study petrochemistry in France.

It was like taking a lightning strike to the head. Not for one second had he imagined that the ministerial reception would have concrete repercussions. He remembered the reply he'd given the minister: agronomy, in Germany. His aspirations hadn't carried much weight, but it was actually just as well they hadn't. Although he couldn't say why, he'd come to love France from school history lessons. And petrochemistry? Why not? It wasn't teaching. But he'd thought of teaching only because he had no other ideas. He'd passed his baccalauréat, and wanted to go further. Moving to Aleppo would take money, and money was something he didn't have. But here he was being offered a grant to go abroad!

Seen another way, this meant being exiled. Still, what was there to keep him here? His father? His grandmother? They didn't even know he'd passed his exams. He'd bumped into one of his half brothers recently and hadn't even said hello. He'd already left them behind, every one of them. The only person he had now was Fadia, and he didn't immediately realize the implications of this possible move. All the time he'd contemplated studying in Aleppo or locally, he'd let himself be drawn into this relationship with her, without really thinking what she meant to him. But now that he was about to leave, he understood just how much she mattered and, by contrast, how little everything else did.

Over time he'd admitted to himself that he was in love with her, but he'd never had the courage to tell her. Deep down, he was afraid she thought of him as just a friend and didn't reciprocate his feelings. Should he risk losing the only person he was close to by suddenly revealing how he felt? And as one procrastination led to the next, as hesitation led to fear, he'd ended up confused about exactly what their relationship was. And yet it was to her and her alone that his thoughts turned now.

Maïouf strolled through the town for the rest of the afternoon, waiting till it was time to see Fadia. He even went as far as the huge ruined ramparts of al-Mansour, stopping for a while in the shade of the open gateway to the road to Baghdad. Legend had it that the great caliph Haroun al-Rachid had walked through this archway when he visited Raqqa. As Maïouf gazed up at the columns and recesses along the wall, he tried to picture the future, France, the West. But before him lay only desert.

* * *

When Fadia appeared at the end of her street, he leapt to his feet. He'd already been waiting some time.

"You've stopped pretending to bump into me by chance," she said with a smile. "Are you trying to compromise me?"

Her eyes shone brightly as Maïouf drew her to one side and, without a word, took out the letter and showed it to her with shaking hands. When Fadia had finished reading it, her face dropped instead of lighting up as Maïouf had expected.

"Are you going to accept it?"

Until then Maïouf hadn't had any doubts about this, but now his heart constricted nervously.

"Yes. Of course . . . well . . . Do you understand?" was all he could mumble.

Fadia took a step back and looked him up and down.

"So we won't see each other anymore?"

What could he tell her? Maïouf made as if to step toward her but she backed away, stopping him in his tracks.

"Of course we will," he managed eventually. "We'll see each other. I'll be home for the holidays . . ."

Fadia said nothing. The smile was still on her face but it was suddenly empty. Maïouf had thought she might share his excitement or at least understand it, and was baffled.

Seeing how upset she was and acutely conscious that he would soon be leaving, Maïouf knew the time had finally come to admit how he felt. If he didn't do it now he'd never have another opportunity. He had to, even if he made a fool of himself. But the pain he detected in Fadia's expression more or less told him he wouldn't look a fool.

"I'll come back for another reason," he said in a choked voice, looking away. "I'll come back because . . . I love you."

Fadia looked up sharply.

"At last," she said.

Her fixed smile had vanished; her eyes were wide. She looked at Maïouf more intently than ever before and, in a clear, perfectly audible voice, said, "Well, I'll wait for you then because I love you too."

As she said these words a strange glow lit up her face, a solemn tender glow Maïouf had never seen before. She handed the letter back to him swiftly and, as on their very first meeting, she disappeared though her front door before he had time to react.

The following day Maïouf and Fadia met on the road to Deir ez-Zor. It was almost nightfall and there was already a coolness in the air. They took a track between two villages, heading out into the desert. The road surface was very uneven, pitted by violent rainstorms, passing herds, and ruts made by the wheels of a cart. The track came to an end on a stony plateau, and in the space of a few minutes it took you from the cultivated banks of the Euphrates to the vastness of desert hills and dunes. Here and there along the way stood crumbling tumuli, their sides eroded with dark holes, but these ancient tombs had been empty a long time. When Maïouf and Fadia reached higher ground, they looked down and saw a spring. They climbed down to watch the water bubble to life at their feet. Fadia told Maïouf that the water in a source has to fight to exist, battling against the sand and stones that drive it back into the ground, away from the sun.

"And yet it's so clear, it shows no trace of this fight, it reflects the sun's rays and gives us a clear view of the stones beneath it. But the sun and stones go on attacking it, trying to stop it from living, so it carries on fighting and it wins. Ever since men have been here to see it, this water has been fit to drink."

Maïouf looked around and noticed strange scattered outcrops of greenery, like tiny velvety tufts of grass. He bent to pick one. It smelled like a peppery version of thyme mixed with sage, bitter but also smooth.

"That's a rare herb," said Fadia, noticing what he was holding. "It doesn't appear very often; you must be lucky. It heals all sorts of pain, stomachaches as well as headaches, and it also helps people sleep when the full moon won't let them."

A slender crescent moon suddenly broke through the red marbling in the sky; night had fallen quickly.

On the way back they hardly dared talk, as if the previous day's confession was too momentous for them. They walked side by side in silence.

26

The bus was meant to be leaving. The driver called impatiently to a young man who was refusing to get in. Of course he was waiting for someone, but everyone's always waiting for someone, and you have to stick to the timetable.

"Just a minute, please . . ."

He saw her. She was wearing a pale-colored skirt, and running. When she saw him she slowed, and by the time she reached him she was walking. When they were very close she put her hand into her bag and took out a small parcel.

"I've brought the book you lent me. I didn't think you'd finished it."

"I . . . I'll bring you a present too," Maïouf stammered, taking the book.

Standing here facing each other, they didn't know what to say. They looked at each other but neither dared do anything.

"So, have you finished?" the driver shouted suddenly. "You'll see your girlfriend again."

Fadia hesitated, then leaned forward quickly and lightly, and kissed Maïouf on the cheek.

Dazzled and happy, he hardly noticed that the driver was grabbing him by the shoulders and dragging him onto the bus. It was when he heard the engine and felt the whole vehicle rattling to life that he realized. He raced down to the rear window. The bus was already pulling away and Fadia's outline melted slowly into the crowd.

27

France is a gray country, Fadia. When I arrived in Paris the sky was low, you could almost touch it. And it was too cold to go out.

In this country the poor are sad too. The poor are sad everywhere. I know that. But it feels like they're sadder here—sadder than in our country, I mean. As if they've lost their dignity. It's the first thing I noticed. After I'd been through passport control I practically walked right into a group of homeless people slumped on the floor. Some men and one woman, all mixed up together, sprawled in a stench of pee! Beggars. One of them had a dog, and that dog looked more human than any of them. All the passengers, airport staff, and policemen avoided them and just walked past like they didn't exist. I looked at them for a long time. In the end they yelled and waved their arms at me, but I didn't understand what they were saying. Insults probably. Because I was looking at them. I was hoping to see gardens, soft golden light on flowers, and I found this heap of destitute people in that big, empty, shiny, clean, scoured arrivals hall, like ghosts trailing their distress around on the marble floors of a palace.

I didn't stay in Paris. I just saw it from the plane, it was a gray cloud. Nothing more. Flaubert's fog. I've been sent to a town called Montpellier, not far from the sea. It rains here too. I was told it was definitely a sunny place, but the Raqqa sun must be tired by the time it gets here. The streets are narrow, the houses low and yellow with red-tiled roofs. If it weren't for the cars absolutely everywhere, I might just about be able to see Raqqa. Just about.

Can you imagine, people here kiss in the street! They're noisy, they wear outlandish clothes, and they do outrageous things. Girls as well as boys. At first I made an effort not to stare. I remembered those beggars and how they reacted. But no one notices anyone else here. I've learned not to be surprised by anything. I've told you about Damascus, well, people's lifestyle has evolved a lot further in France! But they don't look unhappy. I live in student accommodations, a big beige building like those on the outskirts of Aleppo. But the buildings here are clean.

The government told them I was coming, so there was a room for me. A room all to myself! Can you believe it? And it's not on the ground floor. This is the first time I've lived so high up, Fadia. It's like being up a minaret or perched on top of a rampart. The windows look onto a park. It'll be pretty when there's some sun. Sometimes there's a smell of resin in my room, from the trees. Other times there's a smell of salt which apparently comes from the sea, but I haven't seen the sea yet. And you may not believe this but there's running water in my room, even a shower. The first few days I turned the tap on just to watch the water running. I'm over that now. But I shower every evening. I'm ashamed. Well, a bit. But not too much. This country has no concept of thirst. There's water everywhere.

I've met some other Syrians among the students. Not Bedouins. But when you're a long way from home that doesn't matter at all. We're all in exile. What does Badawi mean in France? Who'd understand that? I've made friends with them and they're helping me, teaching me the local ways, how the campus works. They give me advice and even sometimes money for food. I'll get my grant soon, then I'll be independent and it'll be my turn to help them.

I'm enrolled at the faculty of physics and chemistry, and it's much harder than I thought it would be. It's hard following lectures in French so I have to go to the language lab to improve my French. We didn't do much chemistry in school so I'm having to start from scratch. But the most awkward thing is that some of my lecturers are women. Oh, I know, I know, you want to be a teacher too. But, well, no woman's ever told me what to do. The other day one of them ordered me to be quiet. I got up and left. I had to apologize. That's something else I need to learn.

I'm giving you all these details so you get a sense of how alone I feel. Sometimes when I'm sitting working in the evenings I feel sad. I think of Raqqa and its little streets. I think of the desert. And I think of you. Your yellow dress. The people here don't like the Syrians. Syrians or Arabs in general are all Bedouins as far as the French are concerned. But I won't give up. In Raqqa I was proud to be a Bedouin but here I'm not so sure. I'll see it through to the end, even if I have to work twice as hard as the others. I won't let myself be beaten, even if I do have to obey a woman. I'll get my degree. There's no way I'm wasting all those years.

What Maïouf didn't describe in his letter was how he changed his name when he enrolled at the university. Instead of Maïouf—"the abandoned one"—he put Qaher: "the victorious."

28

The end of university came at last. Now that he had his degree, Qaher decided to use this time to go home; he'd been away four years. At first he'd felt homesick but didn't have enough money to buy a ticket, so he'd worked, doing little summer jobs. Nothing had put him off, whether it was washing dishes in a restaurant in Palavas-les-Flots or breaking his back harvesting grapes farther inland. He'd also been a math tutor like so many other students, and had managed to save enough.

He'd chosen a window seat on the plane so he could look at the scenery. All in miniature, he'd seen the mountain range of the Alps, the tortuous relief of the Balkans, Greece, and the great Anatolian plain with its vast buff-colored expanses that looked so like the desert but were in fact fields of wheat. Then, through the clouds, he caught glimpses of the foothills of Mount Lebanon before the plane was finally over Syria. Then he leaned forward and peered slightly anxiously at the panorama before him. Maybe they'd fly over his region, he thought. But he didn't spot any river to act as a reference. The desert gave way to an urban landscape and they landed in Damascus.

Now in a bus on its way to Aleppo, Qaher thought back and realized that when he stepped off the plane, the moment he set foot in the airport, he had a very strange feeling. It was as if all the years he'd spent in this country, *his* country, had been erased by his time in France. It was true he'd grown, and he'd certainly matured, but that wasn't the only explanation. In France he'd to some extent adopted the way westerners think and behave, and back in his own country, it was these sensibilities that whispered in his ear, telling him he was a foreigner. He thought of all the immigrants he'd met in France, the illusions they'd kept alive, and the dreams. Still, he didn't know many who wanted to return to their own countries. That was true of him too: he did care for Syria but like a childhood memory, like a connection he couldn't quite bring himself to break off . . .

At the airport he'd leapt into a taxi as if trying to run away from something, and gone straight to the bus station. There he'd caught the bus to Aleppo, where Fadia would be waiting for him.

Fadia. In the early days he'd written to her regularly, still gripped by his own passion and the memory of their kiss. Then their letters had become less frequent, and the memory had faded and paled before the new world he was discovering. His last letter must have been at least three months ago and he now didn't really know what to think. Of course he'd come back for her more than for his family, for the promise he'd once made her. But their love—which still filled Fadia's letters—now felt to him like a teenage flirtation, and he felt awkward about seeing her again. He thought perhaps he had put down stronger roots elsewhere.

The bus left the main road to cut through the suburbs of Aleppo. Qaher sat up in his seat and looked at the European clothes he was wearing. They were a bit creased from his journey, but certainly distinguished him from the other passengers. Gone were the days of the torn djellaba. And yet, despite these trappings he wore with such pride, the fact that he was coming back a changed person to this country which had so often humiliated and mistreated him made him feel torn between two cultures, the one he was born into and the one he'd adopted. He wished he could keep them both but he couldn't join them together, and felt as if he was watching himself, as if he came from nowhere, with no valid references. He'd turned back into Maïouf, the abandoned one . . .

Fadia was waiting for him. As the bus drew into the huge station car park, he saw her motionless figure. She was standing very upright on the sidewalk, surrounded by other people, wearing a veil over her head and a plain robe that looked dark in the harsh light. She hardly seemed to have changed since Raqqa; she was still as pretty. When the bus stopped and opened its doors, he didn't hurry out but waited for all the other passengers to leave before walking along the gangway. When Fadia saw him at last, she came toward him with some hesitation. As he put his foot to the ground, he waved a hand to indicate he had to get his bag, and went around to the back of the bus. He was putting on a brave face, trying to find something to do to give him a few more minutes before they were actually reunited.

Fadia made her way through the people thronging around the bus and ended up next to him just as the bus driver handed him his suitcase.

"Hello, Maïouf," she said quietly.

"Hello," he said, battling with his bag. "Give me a minute," he added, not looking at her. "I'll just sort this out, then I'm all yours."

Fadia stepped aside.

When he eventually came over to her he was wearing a big smile.

"Fadia, I'm really sorry," he said quickly. "I thought I'd have more time but I have to go back to France in a few days, and I also have to see my family while I'm here, and well . . . I have to leave for Raqqa this evening. There. But we have the whole afternoon and, you know, I'd love it if you showed me around the citadel. I've never visited it. It's now or never. And then afterward we could go to the souk, like we used to in Raqqa. I'll leave this in the baggage lockers, then we can go. Is that OK?"

He'd said this all in one breath, not giving her a chance to interrupt. He was lying of course: if he'd wanted to, he could have spent a couple of days with her in Aleppo. But he dreaded the thought. He hoped that by talking quickly, without stopping or allowing her to stop him, he'd make his story credible and catch Fadia out, forcing her to accept the whole package: visiting the citadel and wandering through the souk as well as his scuttling off that same evening.

He succeeded. Fadia found she couldn't think, couldn't analyze the buzzy behavior of the young man she hadn't seen for four years, couldn't read between the lines of his squalling torrent of words, so she had little choice but to agree.

Qaher and Fadia exchanged news as they walked up toward the fortress, which was on the city's highest hill and dominated it with its sheer bulk. She talked about her studies, announcing with some pride that she would soon qualify as a primary school teacher; but he did most of the talking, describing the West, France, the university, and his plans.

The dry heat of July and the steep climb very soon robbed them of all conversation—they had to save their breath. This enforced silence gave Fadia an opportunity to trawl through her memory for an anecdote or a snippet of information about the building they were visiting. Just as they set off on the walkway that led under the towering entrance porch she finally remembered something.

"Apparently Abraham used to milk a white cow on this hill, and the name of the city actually comes from *halaba*, the Aramaic word for white."

Qaher had been walking ahead of her for some way now, and he turned around to launch into a discussion about religion which drew on a combination of his experiences in Syria and the West. They continued to explore these big general questions as they visited the different parts of the fortress, slipping between groups of tourists but taking a very different kind of interest from theirs. When it was time to leave, though, Fadia said they should see the ramparts, where the views were wonderful. Qaher couldn't refuse.

Up on the ramparts she chose a quiet spot to sit down. She'd actually remembered another bit of history and had made a point of not sharing it with Qaher: the fortress's ramparts were conducive to intimacy and were well-known as a meeting place for lovers. The fact hadn't escaped Qaher, who joined her with considerable misgivings.

They sat in silence, side by side, for some time, each waiting for the other to take the initiative. In the end Fadia gave in. Almost whispering, she asked when he thought he'd be back again. Qaher was ready for this question and replied evasively, implying but not actually stating that he might not come back even though he'd finished his studies, but would have to work in France if the opportunity arose. Either Fadia didn't want to understand, or she didn't think it possible that Maïouf, the Maïouf she had known, might work abroad, and she avoided contemplating this hypothesis. Under the blazing sun, with no shade to protect them, before that endless plain spread before them, she started talking about their letters, the things they'd said to each other, and promised each other. But her increasingly insistent tone of voice and her choice of words confirmed what Qaher had feared: while his love for her seemed to have slowly dwindled with time and the distance between them, he could tell that hers for him had grown and strengthened. What really struck him was how strange it would feel if he came back to Syria. He realized to his own surprise that it wasn't Fadia herself who'd faded from his heart, but his whole past and along with it the country that lay before him, and the desert whose fringes he could see in the distance. And while she continued to remember the past and make plans for the future, he felt more and more uncomfortable: he felt oddly like a foreigner in his own country.

Qaher was suddenly brought back down to earth by what Fadia was saying. She was talking about the child they would have together! Early on in their correspondence, filled with the enthusiasm of love and an acute nostalgia for the earlier days, he'd mentioned wanting to have a child with her. Subsequently, he'd never had the courage to put her right, and she'd carried on talking about it as something that would seal their love. And now here she was talking about it again. Qaher jumped to his feet, unable to bear the misunderstanding any longer.

"It's getting late," he said flatly, not even realizing how boorish he was being. "If we don't leave now we'll never get to the souks."

Fadia was still sitting and she gazed up at him open-mouthed. Qaher grabbed her arm, pulled her to her feet, and dragged her behind him, mumbling a jumble of unconnected nonsense.

They left the citadel and strode down the hillside with Qaher still talking aimlessly, throwing his arms around, and laughing for no reason while Fadia tried desperately to restrain him, get a word in, and bring him back around to the subject that meant so much to her. This went on all the way to the bottom of the hill, all the way to the old town, all the way to the square which was heaving with people.

"Are we there?" asked Qaher, pretending not to know. "Is this the souk?"

"Yes," Fadia murmured, tilting her head down to hide her disappointment because she realized there was no chance of having a private conversation now.

And Qaher was on the move again already.

He rushed off into the labyrinth of little streets overlooked by mosques the color of cool sand, heading down covered walkways, shouting as he cut through the crowds and knocking into people, claiming he'd never have time to see everything. Because he suddenly wanted to explore the whole of the souk, walk through all those courtyards with their refreshing fountains that Fadia knew so well, fountains she'd sat beside these last few years, often dreaming of Qaher. He wanted to see all of the caravanserai along the edge of the souk. And he set off ahead of her, hurrying like a European, wanting to accumulate as many images and impressions as possible before leaving. He even let someone clean his shoes, which had lost their luster on his journey.

When night fell at last and the stalls started closing, Qaher and Fadia realized they'd run out of time to stop and have tea and a meze as they'd promised they would. They had only enough time to get back to the bus station.

While the bus was maneuvering to park in its space alongside the others, Qaher felt he couldn't leave Fadia without giving her some crumb of comfort. She was standing silently beside him, exhausted by their afternoon of walking, and also infinitely saddened—he was in no doubt about that—by his distant behavior and the way he'd avoided answering her questions all afternoon.

When the bus doors opened he leaned toward her and kissed her forehead.

"I'll come back in a few days," he whispered. "I'm going to see my family, then I'll come back. I'll call you."

Fadia looked up. A huge smile lit up her beautiful face.

People were starting to move forward and Qaher went with them, imperceptibly moving away from Fadia, but the smile he'd just glimpsed warmed his heart. As the bus set off he turned to see her still standing among a few other people in the car park, and quite spontaneously blew her a kiss.

29

He'd made up his mind. He would be there a couple of days, two at the most; he'd see his family; then he'd go back to Aleppo and talk to Fadia. Sitting there in that bus, he felt what he actually said to her wouldn't matter. He was a little ashamed of his behavior and could still feel the glow of Fadia's happy smile when he said he'd come back, a smile that he thought he'd forgotten but that had bowled him over. And he told himself that while he was with his family he could think about what their relationship meant. By the time he saw her again he would have reached a decision.

Raqqa isn't very far from Aleppo. The bus was heading farther south to Deir ez-Zor and would take only a few short hours to reach the town where he'd spent his teenage years. Qaher calculated he would be in Raqqa at about eleven in the evening. He briefly pictured himself looking for a hotel room, and it reminded him of the day he'd first arrived, trying to find accommodations for his time at school. The memory made him smile. Still, he decided not to go to a hotel; he'd spend the night in the waiting room at the bus station, among the Bedouin waiting for buses. He felt it would be a good way to reacquaint himself with the realities of a world which for now seemed determined to be out of his reach.

The bus headlights suddenly lit up a vast expanse of water on the left: Lake Hafez al-Assad, through which the Euphrates flowed. Qaher stopped thinking about himself and opened his eyes wide. The Euphrates, *his* river!

The bus traveled along the shores of the lake for several kilometers until the river finally appeared, wide and turbulent as it cut across *his* desert. A medley of images came back to him: "puddles" of sand shimmering in the moonlight he could see if he looked up, his mother, his aunt, the desert, school . . . he closed his eyes and succumbed.

Qaher woke feeling stiff and cramped from the night spent on a wooden bench, and didn't immediately know where he was. It took him a few seconds to remember and he grimaced in spite of himself. He really didn't want to see his grandmother again, or his father, his stepmother, any of them. But he had to. He couldn't avoid it.

Outside, the sun was up, and in that waiting room which was open to the four winds, Qaher was surrounded by people coming and going, calling out to each other or struggling to get to where they were going, one with a goat, another with a hen. He also noticed an old woman sitting facing him two rows of

benches away; she was watching him. The world had come back
to life and he needed to move.

He picked up his bag and went out, struck by the heat and
light. He shielded his eyes and, not really sure what he'd do
with the day, decided to get himself some breakfast. A hawker
had already parked his handcart in a corner on the far side of
the square. Qaher wasted no time before going over to him and
ordering a cup of tea and a few sweet biscuits. He stood there
eating them while he thought.

He could call his father, but there was very little chance
he'd send the truck to pick him up. He could go to the market
in hopes of seeing him there, but that didn't seem like a good
idea. He had terrible memories of the last time they'd met there.
He still had the option of taking the bus as he'd done so often
before, but he was feeling too grown-up today, too old to cope
with all the indignities of that journey, to retrace the steps of his
childhood. In the end he opted for a taxi.

He knew there was a taxi stand nearby. He'd never taken
one but he'd seen others do it. Since childhood he'd been fascinated by this means of transport which felt so inaccessible to
him. He walked across the square and some way up the wide
avenue on the far side, then turned into a side street and headed
for a flattened patch of ground where several cars were waiting.
He nodded to himself. They were all big 1950s models the likes
of which he'd hardly ever seen in France, except in books of
memorabilia. Here they were their owners' pride and joy.

When he approached, the drivers, who'd been breakfast-
ing under a corrugated iron lean-to, all stood up at once. They
were probably drawn to his European clothes but when he
came closer and they recognized him as a Badawi, they were

less enthusiastic. All the drivers usually launched themselves at anyone who arrived, trying to attract a customer, but this time they weren't sure, and this gave Qaher time to choose his car: it would be the black Mercedes at the front of the first row. He walked toward it confidently while he rummaged in his pocket to be sure he had enough money for the fare.

After he'd negotiated a price with the driver who'd sauntered over to him nonchalantly, he sat down on the rear seat. It was in very cracked, bright red leather with a strong smell of cleaning oil. The Mercedes revved smoothly, drew away from its parking place, and set off down the avenue.

Qaher lost himself in contemplation of these views which he knew so well but which somehow felt very far away. Raqqa was passing before him in all its glory—and to think he'd thought this was a big town! Of course everything looks huge to a child, but now that he'd seen the Western world, not only did Raqqa look like a tiny provincial backwater but . . . he tried to find the right expression: it looked like somewhere you'd come to die. Yes, if he had to come back to Raqqa, or even Aleppo, it would feel like dying; he'd languish on his feet.

Just as this thought came to him, the taxi drove out of Raqqa through the ramparts. Beyond the hood of the car, apart from a few construction sites there was nothing but the straight line of the main road with desert on either side all the way to the horizon. A light wind had lifted and the road was dusted with fine sand.

Peering through the smoked glass window from his comfortable seat, Qaher looked at the scenery stretching on either side of the road: an inhospitable, stony plain where only scrub managed to grow, a slightly undulating surface dotted here and there with sand holes whose dangers he knew only too well. He expected memories to come flooding back, expected the edge of the desert to mean something to him. But no. Or rather the only thing this desolate landscape reminded him of was his uncle's trial. Why that memory alone? Why that and not the tents, the houses, the people? He had no idea.

They passed the bus stop he used as a child, then a few minutes later the taxi left the main road to head off into the desert along a potholed sand track. Qaher craned his neck to the right, trying to make out the path he used to take in the days when he was called Maïouf, the one that cut straight across the plain toward the village in the distance. He tried with all his might to see it, to catch sight of its meanders. But he couldn't, and eventually gave up. He felt thwarted, though, and had the strange feeling that his past was reacting to his indifference by eluding him.

All at once he spotted the first houses of his village. The Mercedes was going slowly, its owner keen not to damage it on this track more suited to donkeys than cars. This gave Qaher time to watch the village as it came into view and to think. As the car reached the top of a rise, he tapped the driver's shoulder and asked him to stop.

Qaher sat on the ground looking down. Below him was his father's village with, in the center, that concrete cube of a house he was so proud of. Beyond, on the far side of a barely visible ridge, were his grandmother's village and his mother's grave. What was he here to do? Should he visit his father? Or his grandmother? And what for? To be humiliated—again—by these people who didn't understand anything he was trying to do, or what he was about to achieve, people less welcoming than the desert stretching before him? And yet these people were his family. If he broke all contact with them, he was breaking with his whole past.

The taxi driver had also gotten out of the car, and he gave a little cough. Qaher looked up; he had to make a decision. He looked one last time at the village, his father's house, the desert, this godforsaken, barren place, then got to his feet, gestured to the driver, and opened the back door of the car. The driver looked at him questioningly, and he paused for a moment.

"We're going back," he said coolly. Then, on a sudden impulse, he changed his mind: "No, first there *is* one thing I'd like to do."

The taxi stayed on the road down below. Up on the hillside there was no trace of his mother's grave. Qaher knelt down anyway. He couldn't seem to cry and yet he wished she were there. She and she alone would have been proud of his success; she and she alone would have been happy to see him. He didn't stay long.

He'd made up his mind: he wouldn't stay in Syria a moment longer.

The taxi headed back to Raqqa.

Yes, he was sure now. His life, his future didn't lie here. He no longer belonged to the desert.

On the way back he noticed a flock of sheep grazing the rare outcrops of grass, and that was when childhood memories finally came back to him. But what he saw were images of parties and feasting in which he'd never participated. He remembered the pleasure these occasions had given him as a teenager. Everyone ate traditional mutton, and the brain was kept for guests of honor. He felt no trace of nostalgia, and simply thought, "Soon all that will be over and gone. Soon it will all have been wiped out by oil." He tried to feel remorse for this unkind thought, but didn't succeed.

At the bus station he bought a ticket straight to Damascus. As the clerk handed it to him he suddenly remembered Fadia. Oh well, he thought, he'd write to explain. For now he had to leave, to get back out.

He'd soon be on his way to Abu Dhabi, where he was being taken on as an engineer by an oil company.

30

The tarmac was scorching and the black ribbon of the road melted into the sand dunes in the distance. A few meters ahead, beyond the hood of the car, it hovered nebulously, quivering in the heat, so that, if you gave free rein to your imagination, it was like being on a boat skimming silently over the crests of earthly waves. Clouds of dull gray dust swirled up furiously, then fell away as the heavy vehicle passed, accentuating the impression of being on a boat. But if you looked back you saw a dry, arid landscape, an endless whitish expanse filled with impassive threat.

A charcoal sky stretched across the horizon with oppressive ocher and mauve clouds scudding across it. A sandstorm was brewing deep in the desert. The day suddenly darkened.

The little man in a dark suit sitting beside Qaher leaned toward the window to look out. For a moment he was lost in the folds of desert landscape, then he shifted back into his seat with a satisfied sigh.

"It's been very hot the last few days," he said in the same coolly polite voice he'd used throughout the trip, not even looking at Qaher. "And when the whirlwinds whipping up the sand come together they can produce storms."

He gave the beginning of a humorless smile, nodded his head toward some distant place lost beyond the hills, and resumed his featureless silence. It fell to him, as administrative director for the Company, to initiate new arrivals in the work schedule and the scant perks, which included the desert. He acquitted himself of this chore diligently and with conspicuous indifference even though, deep in his little man psyche, he obviously drew some dubious pleasure from wielding a modicum of power. It had to be said the desert did seem to be a mystery to all these young engineers fresh out of school. He, on the other hand, had been here three years; he knew enough about it to impress them. As for this young boy he'd just collected in Abu Dhabi, this was clearly his first job and he'd probably have to teach him everything.

The day grew darker still. Qaher, who saw little point in replying, wanted to open the window so he could smell the air, something he used to like doing as a child when darkness stole over the desert. It had been sealed shut. He tried a little more forcefully; with no success. The man beside him misinterpreted the gesture and was quick to reassure him.

"Don't worry, we'll be there soon," he said.

Qaher glanced at him surreptitiously. The little man seemed not very concerned, more uninvolved. Nestled nice and safe, deep in the back of the car, he looked at the outside world as if it were a film being projected onto a wide screen. From the look of him, with his impeccable tie and his blandness that touched on nonexistence, Qaher knew in a flash that this man had never dared set foot in the desert he was purporting to tell him about. He even wondered whether he might have had the car windows sealed to stop desert smells from getting in. He was careful not to comment, though.

Qaher ignored the jumbled images of the past that kept coming back to him, memories from a childhood he'd decided to forget: all those sensations and faces and smells. He leaned back against the leather seat and, taking his lead from the little man, affected detachment.

The car raced onward, gobbling potholes and stones on the road, swallowing clouds of sand, even outstripping the thoughts barging into Qaher's head. The metal monster didn't even slow down when it passed animals wandering along the verge, only miraculously missing them every time. The first couple of times Qaher was quite anxious, but he'd stopped worrying about it. Not interested in his traveling companion's occasional pronouncements and no longer fretting about how dark the sky was, he was now lost in contemplation of "something" that had appeared to his right. For some time now he'd been aware of a pipe running parallel to the road, about a hundred meters away. So that's all it took! thought Qaher. A pipe, a simple pipe could do away with the desert and simultaneously relegate his childhood to the realm of a lost era. A pipe, a simple pipe would propel him into the future that he'd chosen, a future made of tubes, pumps, and noise.

It was at this point that the car came out of a blind bend and only just missed a cluster of Bedouin children trying to cross the road. The driver grumbled but made no attempt to slow down. Qaher gasped and spun around to see whether anyone had been hurt. All he could see were the sheep that the children had been leading back to camp; they were skittering over the rocks to get away, terrified by the noise and drag of the passing car.

"Tell the driver to be careful!" Qaher chided, turning to face the front again.

Nestled in his seat, the little man in the dark suit gave no reply. It wasn't until a while later that he deigned to mutter, "Don't worry. It's always the same with you new boys . . . you get in such a state. You'll get over it. A dead Bedouin doesn't matter here. At best, it's one less mouth to feed."

The man took out a handkerchief and wiped the back of his neck. Realizing he needed to justify his cynicism, he added, "The whole country depends on oil production, do you see? So we're not going to trouble ourselves for a handful of nostalgic nomads surviving off a handful of ewes. Personally I don't have anything against them, you know, so long as they don't get in the way of our work . . ."

It grew even darker; it was now almost like nighttime. The bushes they passed grew increasingly gnarled. A tightly packed flight of swallows skimmed past close to the ground. But all this disappeared when the car forked off onto a route that led deep into the desert. Qaher looked up, eager to see the installations, and forgot to reply to the little man in the dark suit.

When Qaher had arrived at the almost insolently clean and modern Abu Dhabi airport the previous day, he'd taken a deep breath, filling his lungs with the hot outside air. It wasn't because he was happy to be back on the soil of his past—in fact the countryside here looked more like a salt lake than the desert as he knew it—but his stomach knotted with a combination of pride and apprehension. A car was waiting for him. A black limousine, not something he'd seen often, even in France. The driver put his bags in the huge trunk, and then set off along the wide, fast-flowing expressway.

When the city appeared on the horizon he was almost dazzled, perhaps because of the sunlight flashing off the sea and the great glass tower blocks. In any event, this light was his first true impression of the United Arab Emirates. The sky here was pure, like the skies Qaher remembered nostalgically.

As they drove into the big modern city, his nostalgia vanished and was replaced by dismay mingled with surprise. The farther the driver took them along those avenues, the more the city shed its Arab identity—at least the Arab identity which Qaher imagined it had but which was due more to the sizzling light in the sky overhead. In the center, the city felt almost Oriental to him. Qaher was unpleasantly struck by how artificial his surroundings were. Of course the oases he'd known as a child had been luxuriant, but they'd never allowed anyone traveling through them to forget they were in the desert. Here in Abu Dhabi, though, the avenues and crossroads were embellished with exuberant vegetation, a carefully maintained, unnatural flora of low shrubs and lilacs and, at intervals, more palm trees than he'd ever seen, to the extent that it was hard to believe he was in the Arabian Peninsula.

The driver took the coast road so Qaher could see the mangrove tract with its intensely blue depths. But instead of enjoying the view, all Qaher could think of were the tankers plying up and down the Persian Gulf behind the spit of land blocking his view.

They left his bags at the hotel and then went to one of the oil company's offices. A little man in a dark suit, a man who

managed to look both self-effacing and oddly arrogant, was waiting for him behind a desk. When Qaher shook his hand—which
he found unpleasantly limp—he suddenly stopped being a pas-
senger: he was here to work. Petrochemistry, the choice that had
been made for him in Damascus.

31

It was a Friday, the beginning of the weekend for Western engineers and a day of prayer for Muslims; he was both. Standing out in the street, he heard the muezzin, and his heart constricted involuntarily, in the viselike grip of memory. His heart beat a little faster and his recollections came to life with new energy. The desert was reclaiming him . . . unless it was something else. He went into the building.

The air-conditioning was on too high, and Qaher shivered as he stepped into the dark blues of the Columbia Café. In a corner of the room a pianist was playing quietly and with earnest intensity. His face was lit by a soft half-light in contrast to the harsh neon glare in the rest of the room. Gaggles of guests from the Beach Hotel were starting to come in. They weren't hard to distinguish from the regulars: they looked more alert and more awkward, and kept in tight groups like tourists in the souk before they surrendered to the pleasure of buying.

Qaher was immediately put off by the artificial chill and superficial atmosphere, and was tempted to go back into the burning heat outside. He had a sudden urge to be in the heavy salty air on the avenue with the light flashing off the sea and the feeling of the sun on his skin, but most of all the blaze of late evening light which reminded him of how as a child he used to run home from school across the desert.

He was about to leave when he saw someone in the middle of the room waving at him wildly. He'd been spotted by David Bensoussan, a young computer analyst of Jewish descent whom Qaher had always found very kind and forthcoming, and reassuringly disillusioned. Bensoussan invited him to join the group sitting at a table drinking, and wouldn't sit down again until Qaher waved back at him with a sigh of resignation.

Qaher immediately regretted what he saw as weakness. Letting the door close behind him, he gestured toward the bar, meaning he had something to sort out before he joined them. A bit longer, just a bit longer . . .

For eight months now he'd been working as an engineer at a network of very rich oil wells in the Habshan region, nearly two hundred kilometers inland from the Persian Gulf. He'd acclimatized faster than most newcomers—everything was already familiar to him—and had established his place on the team, even fitting in with its little ways. But deep down, he felt he was constantly out of step with the others.

When he'd accepted this job, Qaher had decided to devote himself entirely to his work. And he'd stuck to this decision. He didn't see many people, didn't go out much, arrived at work early, and left late. He'd become so isolated that when he did take some leisure time, like this evening, he felt somehow pointless.

Without the power and thrum of the machines at work, all that was left was the company of other men, like those he was with now in hopes they might help him relax.

Of course he got on well with "them," the members of his team, whom he currently called his friends. Still, it had taken only a few weeks for him to realize that things would be the same with "them" here as in France. Perhaps he no longer needed to prove his abilities, but he still had to play his part, know his place. That was the weakness of men: they judged on appearances, unlike machines. In times of doubt, Qaher wondered whether he'd ever find that elusive sense of belonging: a Badawi in Raqqa, a Syrian in France, a foreign worker in the Emirates, he was always a stranger to the people around him. But when optimism wrapped him in its embrace he smiled. After all, what could appearances do compared with cunning? Cunning, the strength he'd inherited from his ancestors, was a distortion of power that fascinated him; it was a sort of technique and one that could be learned. Cunning operated on a deep level; it was an art that he was born to, and it allowed him to get around those who thought him weak. He did this without hypocrisy, though; it was more that it had become a habit, driven by necessity from his earliest childhood until those first years in France. He had a way of never asserting his own importance but always making himself indispensable so that people who wanted nothing to do with him in the beginning would end up recognizing his strengths and asserting his importance for him.

And then, although he didn't notice it happening, the course of his life had been altered by those years in Montpellier spent shrugging off his past and studying. Until he lived in France he had fought to throw off the trappings and prejudices of his people—things that others might call traditions—but all that had been turned on its head. What had looked like rebellion during his childhood had had to be transformed into discipline and conformity, a young Badawi's attempt to fashion himself on the accepted image of a westerner. And he'd won that particular battle. But he was no longer too naive to realize that this victory was only temporary; everything would be temporary for him until he asserted himself in a world that wasn't his own, until he became the master of his own image.

He wasn't there yet. For now he had to carry on playing the game, meeting up with his "friends" for a drink as he did at the end of every week, a ritual that always seemed to go on forever and which did little for him: it involved not coming to life until you'd had three neat bourbons. But Qaher didn't really want to avoid it. So he turned up at these weekly get-togethers in his impeccably pressed suit—he'd learned to perfect his appearance, appearance being a part of cunning.

Knowing he couldn't dawdle at the bar any longer without looking rude, Qaher made up his mind to join his friends. He walked unenthusiastically toward a low table in the middle of the room where four men in shirtsleeves were already lounging in big black leather armchairs, while a diverse clientele bustled and chatted all around them.

32

Qaher drew closer to the low table of lacquered wood embedded with shards of colored glass—halfway between Islamic art and the latest interior design—and saw a lot of drinks on it. The glasses were half-filled with an amber liquid that matched the tones of the table, and they sparkled under the lights. Yet again: bourbon and small olives. This routine was handed down from one generation of engineers to the next and served as a smoke-screen for his colleagues' slow descent into alcoholism. He gave a small smile. As if this was a signal, everyone started talking at once: "Late again!" "We couldn't wait, look!" "How are you? Hey, pull up a chair and come and sit with us!" "So, Qaher, everything under control?" "No work chat, we've all agreed!"

Qaher parried this verbal assault with a modest, "Yes, every-thing's under control."

He moved a chair and parked himself in the space between Bensoussan and Durieux.

"What's happened to you? You look miserable!"

Oxley Brint was British and, from the day he arrived in Abu Dhabi, he'd deemed it his duty to defend the Anglo-Saxon reputation for heavy drinking. Ever since, he had been successfully enlisting his friends in this crusade. This meant that other people's good or bad moods didn't matter much to him, and he was quick to add, "Come on, Qaher, have a bourbon like everyone else!"

Qaher took off his jacket, put it carefully on the back of his chair, sat down, and looked slowly at the others. When he finally grasped that they were waiting for his reply, he muttered self-consciously, "Yes, yes, I'll have a bourbon. As for how I look . . ."

David Bensoussan interrupted him by waving to the diminutive Filipino waiter who was clearing the next table, then turned to him and encouraged him to go on: "So, you were saying, how you look . . ."

"Nothing, it's personal," Qaher said, hoping the others could be satisfied by this evasive reply.

All of a sudden the room was full of noise and people. A group of about twenty had just arrived and were making absolutely sure they were noticed. Men and women who in their humdrum everyday lives were mostly discreet, self-effacing, crippled by scruples and frustrations, went wild here, far from home and disguised as part of a crowd. They were loud and brash, quick to pick arguments, and—worse still—given to unpleasant hysterical laughter. Qaher closed his eyes. Usually these performances irritated him, but not today. He hoped it would distract his so-called friends at least long enough for them to forget the beginning of the conversation they'd just had. With a bit of luck, he thought, he could slip away earlier than usual and lose himself in the thoughts preoccupying him this evening.

Unfortunately, Durieux looked up nonchalantly and raised his voice to be heard above the din.

"What is it? Is it family? Bad news?"

Durieux was also an engineer, but he could just as easily have been a café waiter or a poet: nothing about him revealed why he'd opted for his chosen career. He was one of those who preferred the film evenings at the French Institute to betting at the racetrack and took pride in being different although with a good dollop of affectation. He actually demonstrated a level of intelligence that Qaher respected, but this was coupled with a curiosity that sometimes bordered on indiscretion. That explained why he couldn't pass up an opportunity to find out a bit more about Qaher's private life, particularly as Qaher himself was normally unusually discreet on the subject.

"In a way," Qaher conceded with controlled composure.

"I can't really hear with this noise," Durieux pursued shamelessly. "What? What bad news?"

"No secrets here!" David Bensoussan threw into the mix, laughing, almost drunk.

"I'm not keeping secrets."

The waiter in his white uniform had just put the glass of bourbon on the table along with a plate of olives. Qaher bought some time by taking a gulp of his drink and nibbling on an olive.

"It's to do with a girl."

"A girl!" Alvaro perked up.

To use his own vernacular, Alvaro was a "whole different lemonade" from Durieux. The product of fiercely republican

French and Spanish parents, he'd made a point of being indifferent to all political issues, and had turned his energies to the fairer
sex instead. Poor Alvaro! Here he was languishing in a country
that offered few satisfactions for his desires, a country where
women didn't actually wear the veil—because the Emirates were
liberal—but still had to cover their bodies in heavy fabrics that
gave nothing away. Alvaro tried his luck with female tourists,
with varying degrees of success, and that was partly why he'd
chosen this bar. The thought of additional prey delighted him.

Qaher was about to reply when Brint, who was probably
exasperated by his dithering and was anyway far too busy drinking, raised his glass and yelled, "Here's to you." Then, as he
brought the glass to his lips, he added, "And here's to this girl
of yours, too!"

"You will introduce her to us, won't you?" Alvaro asked
anxiously.

And they all raised their glasses.

The conversation drifted from one thing to another, and eventually ran dry while the big ceiling fan carried on whisking the air
as vigorously as ever. All of them gradually succumbed to a sort
of torpor as one drink led to the next. Foreigners stationed in
the Emirates enjoyed a number of privileges that they eventually
took for granted. They were better paid here than in other places,
benefited from unwarranted comforts and the illusory safety
of a rarefied community, and were therefore often reduced to
indolence and laziness. Qaher knew this, but made the most of
the general restorative lethargy and, forgetting his companions,

sat back comfortably in his chair, picked up his umpteenth drink, and lost himself in thought.

Fadia had written to him, telling him she would be there soon. How had she tracked him down? In his last letter—which was such a long time ago!—he didn't remember mentioning the Emirates; he wasn't even sure he'd been offered this job at the time.

He'd continued his correspondence with her as if carrying out a duty, so he didn't remember it very clearly. It was completely possible that he'd referred to this work in some way, or said how badly he wanted to secure a job like this one, or he could easily have mentioned the name of the Company. Fadia would only have had to do a bit of research . . . She was perfectly capable of that. That's what had attracted him to her: her liveliness, the intelligence brimming in her eyes, always eager to know more, whatever the obstacles. Fadia had written to him, and was coming to see him . . . That was no one's business but his.

33

He'd hoped to get away from them earlier, but here he was still at the table with Durieux, the last of the gang, like two late-night drunks. Brint, Alvaro, and Bensoussan had left, in that order. They'd all, including him, had a lot to drink, but they hadn't talked about his girlfriend again.

As the evening had worn on the place had undergone a transformation, and the air had grown thick with smoke until the ceiling fan struggled to dissipate the dense clouds accumulating around its blades. All it could manage now, in the early hours of the morning, was to tear slowly through the smoke, leaving trails of it hanging over the customers' tired heads, creating gray and white swirls that sank back down, seeping into people's noses, dimming the light, and blurring outlines just as much as the drink did. The customers had changed subtly too. The chirpy, festive tourists wanting a predinner drink had been replaced by couples and more restrained groups; then, imperceptibly, people had started to leave until there were a few lone stragglers left, still at their tables, still nursing their drinks, still gazing bleary-eyed. The Columbia Café was now not even half full and had lost all the comfortable modern appeal it had had at the start of the evening. Qaher had the same sad, fish-out-of-water feeling he'd so often had in the bistro near the Montpellier train station, where he used to go for a solitary cup of coffee when he was heading home late in the evening. Everything reminded him of it, down to the end-of-the-evening noises in the room with the waiters, eager to wrap up their night's work, unsubtly clearing the tables.

"They're closing soon," Durieux said suddenly. "Shall we go?"

Qaher extricated himself from the fug and sat up.

"If you like."

The air outside was humid and the streets were empty. They walked in silence for a while, letting their footsteps lead them to the coast road, and they decided to walk along the seafront. Only the slow slapping sound on the shore and the occasional glint of light on the water indicated they were close to the sea. It was so black and flat in the dark, you could easily miss it.

"Wasn't there something you wanted to talk about?" Durieux asked, tilting his head.

"Me?"

"Don't say there wasn't. I've been watching you for a while. Our get-togethers don't do much for you at the best of times but this evening was worse than ever . . ."

Qaher was relieved he could finally unburden himself of the thing that had been oppressing him all evening but was unsure about broaching a personal subject. He picked up a stone and threw it into the water.

"There's this girl," he said hesitantly. "I knew her in Syria before I went to France."

"And is she just a girl or a girl*friend*?"

Qaher took a big lungful of sea air.

"I don't know. Well, I don't know anymore . . ."

"And is that what's bothering you?"

"In a way, yes. I met her when I was a teenager, at school. I didn't know anything. To be honest I was a bit out of my depth. That school was a big change for me. A whole new world. Well, I'm sure you understand . . . And I was lonely. She was a local, she lived near where I had a room. At first we just bumped into each other sometimes. She was at the same school. We became friends and then we were inseparable. We saw each other a lot. You could say it was with her that I worked out who I am. When I was with her, I felt different, better, do you know what I mean?"

"Maybe." Durieux shrugged.

"When I caught the bus to leave, the one taking me to Damascus, she saw me off, no one else came, just her . . ."

Qaher left his words dangling. He remembered so vividly the kiss Fadia had given him before he left, the kiss he could still feel on his cheek and, along with it, he remembered the promise he hadn't kept. He put his hand to his cheek, right where she'd kissed him. Durieux didn't say anything, and they walked on in silence until Qaher managed to carry on with the story.

"Then I left. We were children at the time. We didn't know what we were doing with our promises and pledges. But we've grown up, we've changed. At least, I've changed."

He didn't dare admit to Durieux that after the first letters following his arrival in France he'd virtually stopped writing to Fadia. He didn't dare tell him he'd gradually put her to one side. And how could he explain changing his name? Or tell him that even though he, Durieux, knew him as Qaher, Fadia remembered him as Maïouf. And how could he tell her? Because he would have to.

"What does she say about all this?" Durieux asked. "How does she react? Did you say she was coming here?"

"I got a letter yesterday. She's a teacher now and she's got an internship in Muscat," Qaher said, waving an arm toward the south. "She wants to see me."

"You didn't answer my question. What about her, has she forgotten like you?"

"I didn't say I'd forgotten!"

"No . . . OK. Let's say, has she changed, then, if you prefer, has she grown up like you?" Durieux conceded, crushing his cigarette with a smile.

No, she hadn't changed. Of course she'd grown up and matured, but she'd forgotten none of her old promises.

"*Every time I feel unsure about something,*" she'd said in her letter, "*every time things get difficult, I think of us and our conversations, the promise I made you and the promise you made me. But maybe you've forgotten all that? I hope not. I've never allowed myself to believe you could forget.*"

He hadn't forgotten, but he'd changed. Or, as he preferred to put it, he'd grown up. He now knew how bitter and arduous life could be, and that childhood dreams had no place in it.

The two men had stopped walking now and were leaning on the railings, looking out blindly over the Persian Gulf that stretched away in front of them.

"What do you think you'll do?" Durieux asked.

"I'm going to see her. She'll be here tomorrow . . . What *can* I do?"

34

"Maïouf?"

Qaher gave an embarrassed smile. Fadia was only meters away, staring at him. He'd recognized her straightaway in the sparse crowd of passengers, but hadn't dared wave at her. Rooted to the spot, he had watched her hesitate, crane her neck, and anxiously scan the faces. But when his eyes met hers, her gaze locked onto his, unblinking. Her eyes were still as clear and bright, undimmed even by the brutal electric light overhead, and their penetrating gaze made him uncomfortable.

"Is it you, Maïouf?"

He resigned himself to stepping forward, just a few hesitant paces. He would have liked to say something but couldn't because of the people all around him. Not that anyone was paying any attention to him: most people were already hurrying toward the exits, and those who weren't were far too busy looking for the drivers who were meant to be meeting them or talking into their cell phones. Still, just knowing they were there made him feel awkward. All of a sudden he was right beside her, within reach, close enough to feel the warmth of her body, to be aware of her smell. He could have touched her. He almost was touching her. He could have kissed her. He looked at her in silence, incapable of uttering a single word, incapable of taking her in his arms. Fadia gave the beginnings of a mischievous smile. She was embarrassed too. She didn't really know what to do either, unsure whether to embrace him or just say hello.

"You've changed, Maïouf. But I still recognize you, you know."

He knew. He grabbed her elbow rather brusquely, took her small suitcase, and then dragged her toward the exit. He was inadvertently taking big strides, walking rather too fast, and only just avoiding bumping into people, desperate to get out of the big echoing arrivals hall as quickly as possible, to be back outside, back in touch with the sky and the earth, and hoping that he'd find the words to greet her once they were outside.

She followed him meekly, almost blindly, a little surprised by his abrupt manner, intimidated by the metamorphosis that had turned him into a man. She didn't seem to have noticed that he hadn't spoken, as if she hadn't yet realized she'd arrived and they'd met up and she was now trotting along behind him. The airport was a soulless ultramodern space with no history, no past, and already no future, a place that depended entirely on oil and would disappear as soon as stocks were exhausted. It looked to her like something from one of the few Western films she'd seen. She hardly even noticed the strange mix of clothing in the crowd, where European suits mingled with expensive djellabas, khanjar daggers with gold watches, headdresses with bare heads, and veiled faces with uncovered, made-up faces.

At last they were out in the fresh air. Facing them were rows of taxis waiting in the shade of palm trees. In the distance the horizon was blocked by the rugged outline of arid black mountains. Where should they go? They came to a standstill, both prey to the same uncertainties. Fadia took this opportunity to release her elbow gently from his grip.

"I need to go to the ministry. You know, to get the papers for my placement. Will you come with me?" she asked in a slightly choked voice.

The sky and the earth had nothing to do with the relief Qaher felt. He took a step away and said with feigned nonchalance, "My car's outside."

"Your voice is just the same!"

"What do you mean?"

"So you've got a car then?"

"Yes. It's lent to me by the Company."

He pointed toward the car park and set off, not so quickly this time. On the way he glanced at the tall glass-fronted building they were passing, and looked at their reflection. Fadia was wearing European clothes, a rather severe anthracite-colored jacket perfectly suited to a new schoolteacher, and it highlighted her slim figure. She'd become a woman. But beneath the woman other people might see, Qaher could still see the clever sensitive girl he'd once known. How many times had they walked side by side like this through the streets of Raqqa? So often that he now couldn't think of the place without thinking of her. He'd always hoped that one day she'd get to see him climbing into his father's truck, but she never had. Now, though, he was taking

her to his own car! Part of his childhood dream was being realized. One last glance at the window before he cut across to the
car park: he thought he looked pretty elegant in the sport-chic
outfit he'd chosen. But the proud young man he saw reflected
here was replaced in his mind by the face he'd seen in the mirror when he shaved that morning. It was a hard face, and the
thought made him wince.

When they reached the car they put Fadia's bag in the trunk,
walked around the vehicle, and climbed in. It was a brand-new
car and smelled of leather. Even though it was early, the sun had
warmed the interior, and this accentuated the usual heavy, acrid,
and—admittedly—unpleasant smell. Qaher pushed a button to
open the windows. As the glass panels glided down with a soft
hiss he remembered the brightly colored buses he used to catch
in Syria, deafening machines that lurched over little back roads.
He'd thought they were so comfortable at the time, but couldn't
think of them now without smiling. He turned to Fadia; she
looked thoughtful too. Before starting the car, Qaher pretended to
make a few adjustments, pointlessly straightening the rearview
mirror. In a way he was trying to prolong this timeless moment:
the two of them, sitting next to each other, like the couple they
could have been. Worried that Fadia might notice his ploy, he
reluctantly turned on the ignition, cut across the expanse of
concrete, and set off along the expressway toward Muscat.

35

Fadia broke the silence.

"How is it, Maïouf?" she asked in a strained voice.

"What?"

"Here. Life here. Is it that different from home?"

Qaher gave a sad little laugh.

"Just look around and you'll understand. The cities here are nothing like Aleppo or Damascus. They're rich, modern, and efficient. Have you ever been to the West?"

"You know I haven't, but I've seen enough reports on TV to know what it's like. I live in Aleppo now, and I've also been to Damascus. What more do you want?" she asked, as if challenging him.

"Nothing, nothing. Anyway, this isn't the West."

"So what is there here, then?"

"Here is everywhere and nowhere. But it doesn't really matter . . ."

They were now speeding along the main road toward Muscat, with the sea occasionally appearing to their left as they turned a corner.

"What *does* matter, Maïouf?"

"Well, what goes on behind the facades, what made all this happen in the middle of the desert. I don't need to tell you about the desert, do I?"

Fadia fiddled with one of the pleats in her skirt.

"There's no point," she replied acerbically. Then, as if regretting betraying her feelings with her tone of voice, she said more softly, "Tell me. What do you mean? Money? I know that these are rich countries, very rich."

Before replying, Qaher sounded his horn at a vehicle in his way, an articulated truck with a long shiny gray oil tank.

"Money isn't just about appearances," he said sententiously. "You'll see. Just look around and you'll know what I mean."

"Right now all I can see is a road with plantations on either side."

"Be patient. What struck me when I first arrived were the glass tower blocks shining in the sunlight. And I can tell you, it's one thing seeing those tower blocks standing against the sky on a screen, and quite another to come face-to-face with them, here, in the middle of nowhere. They shine so brightly they hurt your eyes. Every time I see them, they remind me of the sandbanks along the river near my village. A white glare, so pure you can't look at it. But what really gets me is that these are man-made."

Qaher stepped on the accelerator and overtook a convoy laboring up a hill. As he pulled back in, he scowled in the rearview mirror and muttered something unintelligible. When the road started to drop down into the valley, the city appeared. He reached out one arm.

"There's Muscat."

Fadia leaned forward, peering at the horizon.

"I can't see the tower blocks you're talking about."

The city stretching along the Gulf of Oman was shining, yes, but with the whiteness of limestone interrupted here and there by sandy-colored patches; small, flat-roofed buildings clustered in rows up the rugged hillsides hemmed in by steep mountains with no vegetation: the foothills of al-Hajar. The intense blue of the sea glimmering to her left almost hurt Fadia's eyes.

"This is the sultanate of Oman," Qaher explained. "They stick to tradition here. But if you go to Dubai or Abu Dhabi you'll see the tower blocks and all that."

Fadia studied the city now unfolding before her.

"It doesn't look like Aleppo, that's for sure," she murmured almost to herself. "But basically it's like home. The towns are like oases here too."

"Yes, oases, except the roots of their trees don't grow in the ground but in oil."

Fadia sat back in her seat.

"So, are you an engineer at the moment, Maïouf?"

"I earned my diploma last year," he replied, forking off toward the outskirts of the city.

"So you've succeeded."

"Partly."

Fadia fell silent. And so did Qaher. He didn't want to go on pretending: he knew Fadia wasn't here for a bit of a break or as a tourist. He could tell how artificial all this talk was, all this theorizing about cities and life. The silence went on, and on, painfully. Gusts of air blew in through the open window, whipping his face and making him blink. He regretted coming. And dreaded the moment of truth. The wind, the noise, the stress of this trip. How long would she wait?

"Why did you pretty much stop writing?"

Here we go.

"I don't know. I didn't have time."

It was an inadequate answer, Qaher realized that.

"I had to concentrate on my studies first and foremost. I had to do well, you know. I had to work really hard."

And this was partly true. He'd had to learn to reason in a different way, to think and react like someone in control of things rather than subjected to them. He hadn't forgotten Fadia, but she'd become somehow blurred along with Syria itself and, apart from his brief trip to Aleppo, he'd never set foot back there. Every year was more difficult than the last, and he'd thrown off all traces of his past one by one, like dead skins sloughed off by a snake. And Fadia along with them.

"I'm not the little boy you knew in Raqqa."

"I'm not the girl you said good-bye to at the bus stop, either, you know. Do you remember? *I* haven't forgotten."

When Qaher didn't reply, she added, "And do you remember our conversation on the ramparts of the citadel?"

As Fadia asked this question, Qaher left the coast road to drive into the city itself. The increased traffic and the need to concentrate fully on driving seemed to him like good excuses not to answer. He drove around a sixteenth-century fort, and big road signs with wording in English and in Arabic indicated different routes. He needed to head south.

As they drove past a tall tower, Qaher nodded to Fadia. In Raqqa the town center was arranged around the clock tower, and the bus station that had witnessed their good-byes was at the foot of that tower. Fadia smiled. Qaher thought her smile looked sad, and was aware she was waiting for an answer. Every passing minute played against him and betrayed his indecision, but he couldn't make up his mind to formulate an answer. He could guess what Fadia was thinking: she wanted to know whether he'd ever come home. A question he himself had eventually shelved, thinking time would make the decision for him. But here it was rearing its head again.

When Qaher stopped the car outside the ministerial building he still hadn't replied. Fadia checked her papers.

"You don't have to come with me."

"Go in. I'll wait. I've taken the day off."

She got out of the car, and he watched her disappear, swallowed up by the spanking new building. He batted his hand to drive away a surge of nostalgia. No, he wouldn't go in after her.

36

Outside, the night shone with a thousand fires. The derricks stood at regular intervals, forming a grid over part of the desert: Sector 8 in the huge oil field where Qaher worked. With their red and white lights in the cool of the night, they were a reminder of a mysterious collaboration between man and the earth. Chimney pipes rising up in the night sky occasionally emitted tongues of flame. Drilling arms nodded rhythmically, slowly rising and falling, leaning tenderly toward the earth in a mimicking of a courtship display. From time to time two beams of white light appeared, probing the sky or plunging down ravines: the headlights of a jeep cutting across the oil field. Everything here was alive.

Qaher particularly liked these solitary evenings when the darkness handed the place over to the machines, and men were few and far between. During the day, all you saw were ungainly constructions standing in the crushing heat and the dust, metallic structures with pistons beating the earth, machines which needed constant monitoring—an exhausting, thankless task. During the day, you could see the electric fences protecting the site, and drawing attention to the danger, to the whiff of money, and to the violation of open spaces.

But at night! Darkness created a distinctive kind of intimacy. The stigmata seen in daylight were barely visible. When men and beasts were asleep, all the detractions of technology faded. Even power became harmonious, found some legitimacy. Qaher was here, no longer to monitor, like a slave, but to watch over his domain, like an owner. The risks may well have been higher because nocturnal incidents were more difficult to manage, but this harmony, this feeling of reconciliation with the desert, meant he could be subsumed into the vast machine, become a part of it. If he reached out his hand he even thought he could feel it living.

It could be said that Qaher had been reunited with the desert, but for him the desert was only a secondary factor in his new circumstances. What mattered most to him was what lay at the end of the road: the huge oil-producing complex.

He was immediately aware of its power, a vast, intense, tangible power which bent thousands of people and machines to its will, making them work to its rhythm, with the same aims, pummeling the ground. As a child, he'd suspected this sort of power existed from the mechanical purring of his father's truck, from the oil lamps with which his father flooded his guests with light to command respect and parade his wealth, and from the sheer noise of the construction site erecting Raqqa's law courts, where justice was counted out in banknotes. Here, though, he'd realized how much greater that power was than in his dreams. If power was organized, planned, efficient, and given free rein, it proved capable of prospecting the earth and delving into its entrails. He'd had a taste of this power. He'd been collaborating with it for eight months, it had absorbed him, he was a part of it. More so with every passing day.

The overseer's room was behind a hillock. He parked his jeep in a dip in the ground, cut the engine, and climbed out. He felt sheltered here, at one with the hammering he could feel reverberating beneath his feet.

He had no desire to be hit by the smell of coffee and hot plastic that always pervaded the prefabricated buildings, no desire to inhale the petrochemistry gases that regularly hung over the place despite the technicians' best efforts. Not yet. He'd read Proust at school: oil and bourbon would definitely be his "madeleine." But for now he felt a new harmony with the desert, and he didn't want to disrupt that at any price. If only he could find the words to communicate all this to Fadia! He leaned against the still warm hood of the car and all at once realized he'd never been into the desert with her. They'd really seen only the streets of Raqqa together. One time they went as far as the outskirts of the city, to the ramparts of al-Mansour. The outskirts, no farther. As if the desert had been a frontier, a world in which Fadia didn't belong.

He took a deep breath, picked up a handful of sand and let it sift through his fingers, then leaned against the hood again. It didn't make any sense. And yet he couldn't picture Fadia here, beside him; the desert wasn't where she belonged. It was as if there were two separate worlds, and Qaher couldn't work out whether he belonged in either of them.

The small device he wore on his belt started vibrating. He was being paged. He took a few steps and the thing carried on vibrating, so he unclipped it and pressed a button to indicate that he'd received the message. He lingered there a moment longer, then turned back and sat reluctantly at the wheel of the jeep, started the ignition, put it in gear, and drove back up the sandy slope. The dull thudding in the ground melted into the throb of the engine.

37

The camel sprawling on the ground made Qaher uncomfortable —not the animal itself but what it represented. Fadia had been strolling around it for a while, like any other tourist, occasionally leaning toward the animal to stroke it and scratch its coarse coat. You'd have thought both of them, Fadia and the camel, were trying to taunt him. They made a strange pair, as if artificially playing their allotted roles in this abstract setting. Qaher ran his tongue over his lips. Night was falling, they'd already visited four of the villages around the vast oasis, this was the fifth.

A red sun was setting the tops of the dunes alight. It would have been magnificent were it not for that aftertaste of fakery, and Qaher's overriding urge to get away. The manicured space with its too-green grass put him on edge. Why had Fadia insisted on coming here? He knew at a glance it would be a disappointment, and every moment spent here was proving him right. It was so obvious: Fadia, the camel, the grass, the wind, the light, the noisy tourists pouring out of air-conditioned coaches, the locals, the way the place was laid out—every element was a lie, conjuring a borrowed reality. OK, yes the glimmering orange-and-gold wall enclosing the plain with its lush green vegetation was probably very beautiful, and the terraces of date palms promised plenty of sweet fruit. Except what was *real* about all this? Most people could be fooled. But not Qaher. He was too familiar with the Bedouins' living conditions, the harshness, even the oppression, to accept this counterfeit version. All they needed now was a nomadic tribe to appear on the crest of the dunes, black silhouettes against a scarlet sky advancing slowly toward the water, for the illusion to be perfect!

Fadia had decided to spend the day in the area. Qaher didn't know Liwa and had accepted, thinking they might be able to make a detour past the oil fields to the north on the way back.

Seen like this, desert life might look idyllic: terraces of greenery on the slopes, palm orchards in the valleys, an abundance of water drawn from wells or pumped from storage tanks, the incandescent sun and the comparative cool inside the tents. Was she trying to convince him of this by dragging him here? She knew where he came from, she knew him, she couldn't not know that this set-dressing would end up irritating him.

The desert was hostility that had to be overcome; only someone with no experience of it could believe otherwise. The Bedouin had gained all their strength from their battle with the desert, definitely not from its loveliness. They'd tamed it in their own way, but knew it was still as dangerous as a sleeping snake. And yet he was no longer even drawn to the nomads' fierce arrogance—yes, Fadia should have realized that too. He'd learned another way of taming the desert, not as picturesque as the one that Liwa illustrated, more arduous, but more modern, more *real*. Of course the tourist coaches didn't visit the boreholes, but without them, this picture-postcard place Fadia had taken him to couldn't even exist. And then there were all the little details he'd noticed, like televisions in the tents, the pump drawing water from the well, and the clearly delineated road used by trucks delivering hay. Nomadic life was a memory here, an image. Fadia should have known that. What was she trying to tell him?

She lingered next to the tame camel. Under the shade of an awning an old man smoked a cigarette as he stitched a harness. He looked timeless, sitting there on his carpet with his face burnished by the wind; he could easily have lived in Medina in the sixth century. If you'd asked he might even have told you about Mohammed's armies. Qaher was musing about this when a European rudely asked him to move aside so he could photograph the old man. Everything was ruined here, even dreams, he thought.

A little girl wearing a rather dirty, torn djellaba had latched onto Fadia. She must have been about ten. Her cropped tousled hair made her look open and honest. She wore a silver earring which shone brightly against her dark skin. She was holding out her hand. Fadia, who'd abandoned the motionless camel, had approached her and seemed to be talking to her. In one swift move, Qaher went over to them and brusquely told the child to go away. The girl opened her eyes wide. He repeated what he'd said, his face even harder, almost threatening. When the child didn't move, he turned away and, without a word, dragged Fadia back to the car with him, despite her protests.

"Why did you do that?" Fadia asked when Qaher let go of her to get into the car.

"She shouldn't be begging," he said curtly.

"She just wanted to feel my dress!"

"There are lots of ways of begging, Fadia. Let's go back, I don't want to talk about this."

38

The horizon was lit up by flames brighter than the setting sun. The evening sky quivered with an unaccustomed heat haze. The wailing sirens carried a long way, an exaggeratedly long way, making them frightening and absurd in this place empty of human or animal life. Cohorts of vehicles sped, all lights blazing, along what was usually such a quiet road. Jeeps, water tankers, ambulances, fire engines. Like a swarm of locusts, they descended on the site of the fire.

One blood-red truck had toppled into a ditch, and there was a cluster of activity around it, an ambulance with its blue-and-white flashing light, sparks flying where the angle-grinder met steel, frantic shouts from those trying to free the occupants, but none of this seemed to stop the furious pace of vehicles whistling past the scene in a cloud of dust.

Because there was an emergency. Toward the end of the afternoon, one of the wells in Sector 8 had blown up, although no one yet knew why. For several hours now a huge fire had been dancing above it, a diabolical bacchanal sending up great gusts of flame and threatening the rest of the plant, which it illuminated with its deadly orange glow.

The heat near the center of the fire was unbearable. Despite their fireproof suits, the firefighters shielded their faces with their arms as they approached. Several of them had already been evacuated, smothered when a sudden wind change blasted them with an acrid cloud of burning oil. Worse than the heat, the toxic fumes, and the sickening smell was the noise. A powerful boom, a deep growl that smothered everything else. Anyone who could get close to the geyser of flame heard it as a roar of anger and revenge unleashed by the entrails of the earth, and set to go on forever.

The plant was lit up as if in full daylight. The huge oil tanks and steel pipes, the blocks of concrete and prefabricated buildings—all that inhuman architecture which had dug its roots into the vast expanses of the desert—looked otherworldly in the huge squalls of fire.

After the panic of the first few hours, despondency had set in inside the huts. Particularly among the engineers. The unthinkable had struck. The accident they were responsible for preventing, the accident they were paid to avoid, had happened. What sort of mistake had triggered it? Who was responsible? Because they knew that the Company would be less interested in the financial losses, less interested in injured employees, or even dead ones, than in finding out who was responsible. No point blaming unforeseen circumstances. In this world of perfect efficiency, that was the very last thing you could cite. And even after an inquiry determined it really had been an act of fate, someone would still have to pay. For sure. They could all be blamed for something. Is there any job that involves no risk?

Some had only just woken. Still half asleep, they watched through the red glow of their windows as the catastrophic fire raged over the complex like a hungry monster. If they'd had any religious convictions, they'd have prayed, but they didn't have that succor. They could only watch, powerless, as the firemen and ground staff waged their battle. No one had the heart to speak.

All of a sudden there was an explosion. A jeep had come too close to the fire and a gust of wind had blown flames over it. The three occupants hadn't had time to react. Trapped in a firestorm, they didn't manage to get out before the fuel tank exploded like a watermelon, spattering steel, body parts, and blood. Fragments of twisted metal and severed limbs flew up into the sky, then thudded down, digging into the ground. After a short but violent struggle, some firefighters managed to extricate what was left of the charred bodies. These remains were wrapped in white sheets and laid down behind the hospital tent; there wasn't time to do any more for them because the fire was growing. Exhausted workers gathered out of harm's way, gazing despairingly as the well that they'd toiled over for so many hours twisted, swayed, and broke up in the blaze.

Dawn was still a long way off and no one could see the fire being brought under control before then. The thousands of liters of water being poured over the blaze would never get the better of it. They knew that. Only the blast of a carefully planned explosion could put out the flames. And even then the explosives experts would need to get close enough to set their charges. This would have to happen later, though; for now they were pouring on water to stop the fire from spreading. They'd seen fires spread to other wells before, and that's what they dreaded now. They battled to avoid that, but the flames were so powerful they doubted they'd succeed.

On a small hill to the north of the complex, a cluster of men, women, and children sat in silence on carpets laid on the ground, and watched the agitation in the plain below. The Bedouin had come to watch the show.

39

Qaher had thrown his car onto the narrow dirt road, hurtling along mindlessly, for the pleasure of speed or perhaps simply because he felt hemmed in by the darkness. He'd driven all the way with his jaws clamped, concentrating on the engine sound, trying in vain to hear through it to the crunch of sand and the thrum of the wheels. Fadia had had to settle for looking straight ahead and not uttering a word. They'd left Liwa in a glum mood without mentioning the incident with the little girl.

Night had fallen as they left the expressway at Hamim and turned onto the track. Fadia was tired and had turned down the dinner he'd offered. It was a long way back to Muscat; he hadn't insisted. For a long time the car's headlights lit up only a monotonous series of ridges, then they dropped down toward the sea and habitation.

They were just getting to the first of the city's avenues when Fadia broke the silence.

"I don't understand what got into you earlier," she said, not turning her head. "With that little girl, I mean."

Qaher's hands tensed on the steering wheel; he'd been expecting something like this. But that didn't put Fadia off: she stared at the road ahead and kept talking in a voice that sounded muted and distant to Qaher. Not physically distant, but it seemed to be coming to him across a distance of time, a voice from the past that was drawing him back to the past. She was talking reproachfully, comparing him with the boy he'd once been, reminding him that in Raqqa he'd claimed to hate injustice, and preferred to understand than to judge, but now—now that he was an engineer working for a Western organization at an oil complex—he thought he could get away with being snappy and contemptuous. She disapproved of what he'd become; she thought that he was denying his true nature, that trying to belong to two worlds as different as the desert and the Western world wasn't doing him any good, was turning him into a rootless stray.

Qaher listened to her recriminations before eventually reacting as he was negotiating a crossroads.

"What's all that got to do with what just happened?" he asked, raising his hand angrily from the steering wheel.

He couldn't see the connection, didn't want to see one. He thought Fadia was trying to find a way to express what she'd felt all these years but had never actually vocalized till now. Her reply—"It's the same thing. But you've forgotten everything."—wasn't really a reply at all, and it only confirmed his suspicions, convincing him that he really did have to talk now. He shouldn't have retreated into silence as he had since they left Liwa.

And so, still half concentrating on road signs, he started explaining himself. He wanted to do it without getting angry;

he didn't actually feel angry; he was just wearied by so much misunderstanding. He tried to be calm, almost methodical. No, he hadn't forgotten anything. Not the law courts in Raqqa, nor his uncle's fate, nor the humiliations he himself had suffered. None of it. He still remembered that fat jowly judge, his father's contempt, his stepmother's scheming, the spitefulness of so many people. But what was the point of going back over all that? He wasn't in Raqqa now. He wasn't the little Badawi everyone could make fun of any longer. It was true, he was fascinated by power, but it had already fascinated him as a child, and it had intimidated him too—particularly because it seemed so inaccessible. As an engineer, he now had access to it and reaped its benefits. What was wrong with that? It hadn't made him cynical as she was implying it had.

Lit by the orange glow of successive streetlights along the avenue, he tried to explain to Fadia that, even though strength and power may have hurt him in Raqqa, that was because it had been the strength of the weak. True strength was sure of itself, it was productive, and his work . . .

"Do you remember the letters you wrote to me when you arrived in France?" Fadia cut in, harshly interrupting the argument he was developing.

Qaher didn't reply straightaway, and silence descended on them again. This time Fadia did nothing to break it. She waited. The avenue they were driving along was very well lit, and there was hardly any traffic on it. Lights shimmered all the way down it: orange, green, yellow, and white. Catching sight of a large building ahead, Qaher knew they were on the right road at last, and they'd soon be there. The letters . . . yes, he remembered. Not really thinking what he was saying, he muttered something that could have sounded like "Yes," and which Fadia interpreted as acknowledgement.

"And do you remember talking about a child in those letters?" she asked.

This caught Qaher unawares.

"Yes. Of course. I . . ."

"About *our* child?" She insisted, turning toward him and staring at him intently, making him feel uncomfortable. He almost stopped the car so that, once and for all, he could give her his endlessly deferred explanations, but Fadia had more to say.

He could have been irritated by these constant reminders of the past, by her unwillingness to listen to what he had to say. But, as he looked at her out of the corner of his eye, it felt strange having her there, in that car lit up by those multicolored lights, easing along that modern avenue which occasionally afforded glimpses of the desert close by. She wasn't wearing a shawl and her luxuriant hair framed her face, giving her a whole new dimension.

"I was scared, you know," she said. "Scared to come here. Scared I'd find a foreigner, a stranger. Last time I saw you"— he opened his mouth to speak but she put a hand up to stop him—"Yes, I know, you wrote to explain why you didn't go back to Aleppo. But what difference did that make? Since you left, I mean since you left the first time, not one day, not one hour has gone by when I haven't thought of you. Every morning I'd go to see the mail. Every morning, despite your silence, I hoped I'd get a letter. Every morning!"

Qaher had accelerated without realizing it. He had no answers to these recriminations. He was well aware that he'd wronged her, and it was a wrong he'd tried to avoid by talking about power and work. He knew he'd always made a point of not thinking about it. As he often did, he'd convinced himself things would sort themselves out on their own, and Fadia's love would fade and die. But that's not what had happened, and there wasn't much point saying he regretted that. It wouldn't help, so he didn't say anything.

40

"Stop playing with me, Maïouf!" she cried suddenly.

All the arguments he'd prepared about the past—about time, his childhood, himself, and her—they all collapsed in a flash. All that reasoning was valid for the young girl he remembered. But when he'd turned to look at her in the car just now he'd seen a woman living and breathing beside him, a woman in whom he barely recognized the Fadia he'd loved, a woman made all the more mysterious by the half-light. He screwed up his eyes involuntarily. For a moment the world around him disappeared. He'd opened his mouth to speak but just stood there, his words still unspoken. After what felt like an eternity he eventually mumbled a few words, dredging them up from somewhere.

"Give me some time."

"Time to do what, Maïouf?"

A shadow appeared in the entrance hall, attracting his attention. The woman on duty had come out of her booth and busied herself around a table. She was clearly preparing to close up for the night, and probably had to tidy the mess left by students.

"She's going to lock up, I can't stay out," said Fadia. "Let's meet tomorrow."

"Yes," Qaher said, feeling the situation was beyond him.

"Tomorrow," Fadia said again, and she disappeared into the dim light.

41

Qaher had taken a room for the night in one of the thankless hotels along the city's seafront, a low-slung, almost anonymous building which nevertheless had a reasonably presentable interior. This traditional-looking city still showed signs of its seafaring past, of the trade and commercial fishing that had kept it alive until the ground surrendered up its wealth, and when Qaher arrived he'd gone, without thinking, to the first hotel he found. Over time he had grown used to a degree of comfort, but Fadia and her retinue of memories had reminded him of the life he'd known in his grandmother's cob house, and the evenings he'd spent in tents on feast days; and he had decided this hotel's services would be perfectly adequate. Another detail here reminded him of Syria: portraits of the sultan in pride of place in the reception area, like images of the president on the walls of every little shop in Raqqa.

The streets were empty and he'd driven quickly till he reached the network of little roads leading down to the port. He could now see the square white building at the end of the avenue. On the way here, thousands of thoughts had sprung to life in his mind. After Fadia had left he'd been furious with himself, furious because he hadn't explained himself, but mostly because he was now so confused. But it wasn't long before he thought about the last thing he'd said, and Fadia's conspiratorial smile.

Time. What did he mean by that? Time to come back to her? Did that mean he wanted to get back together with her? True, he hadn't really looked at her since she stepped off the plane. Also true that he'd been prepared to notice only how she'd changed on the outside—until this evening, when her face had appeared to him in that shifting light inside the car, and in her face he'd seen how much of a woman she'd become. Was he falling in love with Fadia all over again? Could this old relationship be rekindled after everything he'd seen, and everything he'd left behind?

Then he remembered the early days when they first met. Fadia was the only person who accepted him for who he was, a Badawi with no family. And he'd been hurting her, for all these years.

He should have written to her more often. Yes, probably. He'd thought he would be able to drive her out of his mind, park their little relationship in some recess of his memory. But he wasn't so sure now.

He remembered the smile she had given him as she stepped out of his car. A glorious smile. He'd never told her she had an adorable smile. The smile of a woman shaped by the gods to be happy, which is just what he'd thought the first time he'd seen her. She had once asked him whether he thought she was pretty, and he couldn't remember how he'd answered. But as he drove along the road toward his hotel, he knew how he would answer now. She was more than that. She was the sort of person you'd want to . . . no, no, you wouldn't want to save her, but you'd want to see her happy, that was all.

She'd said in her letters that he loved her but didn't dare admit it. Did thinking about her as a woman who deserved to be happy constitute loving her?

He'd driven all the way to the hotel while he mulled over all these ideas, and more, plenty more.

Qaher parked his car on the seafront and took a deep breath. He gathered all these disparate thoughts, and put them into some sort of order until he reached a conclusion: if loving a woman meant feeling the distress he was experiencing, if loving a woman meant knowing—as he now knew for sure—that she occupied the deepest recesses of his being, well then, yes, he had to admit he loved Fadia.

Strangely, Qaher acknowledged this "revelation" calmly. He felt as if a knot had been unraveled. He sat in his car for a moment with a half smile hovering on his lips, before eventually making up his mind to get out. The air outside was warm. Qaher walked slowly over to the hotel, contemplating his new-found conviction.

Leaving behind the night with its neon streetlights, he went through the big glass door, which parted silently, as if bowing to him; then he crossed the hall with its soft carpet and opted for the stairs instead of the elevator. A new energy pervaded him, an energy which dispelled the power he'd confronted until so recently. Tomorrow he would see Fadia again. Tomorrow he would talk to her. He would tell her what was on his mind, and in his heart.

42

It was a stupid situation. It was nearly seven in the evening and, after the most ridiculous day of his life, Qaher still had to wait for his fate to be decided. It had all started the night before when he stepped into his hotel room, just as hope had brought some warmth back into his heart. He'd seen a tightly folded note on his bedside table, an official missive from the Company—which had searched every hotel in the city—to tell him there'd been an incident in Sector 8, his sector, and to summon him back to work as soon as possible, even that very night. Still feeling euphoric, he hadn't thought this instruction strange: an inconvenience, a lot of traveling, no more than that. So he'd packed up his things, trying vaguely to imagine what could have gone wrong, and hoping he could settle the problem swiftly. Then he'd raced off, not even taking the time to contact Fadia. How could he have done so, anyway? The switchboard at her halls was not manned twenty-four hours a day.

That night as he drove along the coast and then inland, he'd been obsessed with one thought: getting back in time to meet her where they'd agreed to meet. And now that he had plenty of time to himself—an eternity—he tried to picture Fadia in his mind's eye. Not that he didn't know what she looked like; he just wanted to go on and on exploring, contemplating in minute detail the face of the secret, enigmatic Fadia he'd discovered earlier that evening. Perhaps it would only prolong the state he was in . . . but then again he had no desire to end it. He should have been worrying about why the Company had summoned him in the middle of the night; but he didn't think about that. He couldn't tear himself away from the excitement of love. He wanted to think of Fadia and nothing else. In order to conjure a mental picture of her, he combined the very clear memory he had of her face as a teenager along with her face as the woman she'd become. But despite all his efforts, Fadia's features started dancing before his eyes, scattering over the surrounding countryside lit by his headlights, jumbling themselves up; it was as if this longed-for face was toying with him. Only the halo of hair remained constant, and he remembered Omar Khayyam's words:

> *You, whose face was used to fashion lilies, oh my lovely!*
> *You, whose beauty is ever a faithful image, oh my lovely!*
> *The King of Babylon invented the game of chess*
> *Based on your knowing ways, oh my lovely!*

It was like a revelation. He was calling on the poets—having neglected them terribly in the last few years—to crystallize her dancing features. Now, standing in a corridor, he couldn't remember all the verses that had come back to him as he drove along but, thanks to the poets, he'd managed to recall all the elements of Fadia's face, one by one: her thick hair, her dark eyes, her clearly defined cheekbones, her fine nose, which had curved slightly as she'd matured, her pure lips always ready to smile, her tidy little chin, her whole face, in fact. And, as they like to say in Arabia, it was as beautiful as the moon. He'd forgotten the verses that had helped him reconstitute her face, all except the last, because he'd sung and shouted, whispered and chanted that particular one until the end of his journey. It was a couplet from one of the tales in the *Thousand and One Nights*, tales he'd learned as a child, between the desert and Raqqa, and now knew almost by heart.

> *Whether near or far, your face*
> *And your name are always on my lips.*

These two lines had stayed with him and were still resonating inside his head, only much more softly because while he'd been driving, the idea of her being far away had been just a poetic turn of phrase, but as he stood waiting in that corridor lit day and night by harsh electric bulbs, it was starting to become a bitter reality.

And yet he was still thinking of Fadia, not the men discussing his fate on the other side of the door. Fadia who must be waiting for him in vain, Fadia who he needed to talk to, *whose tousled hair had so burned his heart*, as the Persian poet put it.

As he'd drawn near to the scene of the fire, his arms and legs stiff from so much driving, the night still glowed red from the blazing flames. He was stopped by orderlies manning a safety perimeter. At the point where they'd stopped him he couldn't see much of the devastation being wrought, but he could tell it was bad from the stress on their faces, the frequent walkie-talkie conversations they had, and the snatches of information they gave him. After a lot of discussion, one of them sent him to an area that was out of danger, toward the south of the complex, back the way he'd come behind the hills. They were expecting him there.

Thoroughly exhausted and with his head still full of thoughts, Qaher was fairly ill-tempered as he retraced his steps. He had to drive another good fifteen minutes through the desert over an almost impassable, rutted track before reaching the assembly point. It was an oil field like Sector 8 but on a smaller scale and, more important, it was isolated. Everything seemed calm, ordinary, routine. A far cry from the tension he'd just witnessed. After he cut the engine, Qaher sat for a moment listening to the strange whistling sound of the desert; then he went into the building. But he didn't find any of the people he thought would be waiting to see him.

The door opened to reveal the usual team of guards. They were waiting for him. An engineer in white overalls came to greet him, briefly abandoning his control panel. He showed Qaher into a staff break room and asked him to wait while he got in touch with the managers. What else could Qaher do? He waited.

The room was in a prefabricated building, an exact replica of the one in which he'd spent the last few months. Qaher noticed that familiar smell, a combination of oil and plastic, and he had a cup of the same thin, scalding coffee in his hand; for a moment it felt as if the time he'd spent with Fadia was aeons ago, as if it had been propelled back into a misty, dreamlike past.

But the illusion didn't last. Tiredness and anxiety took over. To kill time and because this was his first proper opportunity, he started thinking seriously about what had brought him here. For starters, he couldn't really see why this needed sorting out in the middle of the night. What needed sorting out, anyway? Qaher couldn't understand why they needed him there so urgently, and certainly couldn't see why they'd now kept him waiting for nearly an hour. The fire had started while he was away; he was in no way responsible for the disaster. As for the firemen and their battle to overcome it, there was nothing in his skill set to help them. Unless he was simply the chosen victim. The duality he felt inside himself, the notion—or perhaps he should say the fact—of being an Arab among Europeans and a European among Arabs could very easily turn against him. Of the engineers who worked at Sector 8, he was the only one of his kind. Could that be why he'd been summoned?

When he heard footsteps outside, Qaher got to his feet. The engineer appeared in the doorway, looking embarrassed: he hadn't managed to get hold of the investigators. It was probably only a matter of time, but Qaher would have to keep waiting. He didn't know any more than that. Qaher wanted to call Durieux and Bensoussan in the hope that they could shed some light on things. The engineer refused to let him. Well, of course, he didn't explicitly forbid him, but he made such a fuss that Qaher grasped it would be better if he didn't contact his colleagues before talking to the investigators. That was when Qaher realized he might not be able to get away quickly. He let the engineer go back to work, and sat down on a folding chair, pulling his jacket tightly around his neck.

Stranded in that anonymous room in a prefabricated build-ing, sitting on an uncomfortable chair with a now cold cup of coffee in his hand, he tried to think of Fadia, but the enthusiasm that had surged through him in Muscat had faded. And nothing about his present surroundings was likely to revive it. Fear had insinuated itself into his mind. Wasn't there something in the air and, more particularly, in the imperious tone of that note, wasn't there a whiff, a vibe, a nervous tension which reminded him unpleasantly of that court case in Raqqa? Right now, the waiting, the contempt with which he was being treated, the ridiculous way he'd made himself available, not to mention the fact that it was night and he hadn't been allowed to make any phone calls, made him feel it was *his* trial going on. And wedged into that chair, dazed by the neon lights, he couldn't help thinking his sentence had already begun.

Qaher shook off his lethargy and walked out of the building, hoping he'd be able to gather his thoughts. He climbed up a hillock to look out over the installations with their derricks and hundreds of lights dotted across the desert. The anticipated thrill had been lost along the way. The scene didn't light up before his eyes. When he scuffed the ground with his foot, he just loosened the earth, the desert sand. He sat down. The desert, the darkness, the hillock . . . it all reminded him of something he couldn't pinpoint. Instead of Fadia's face, which he so wanted to see, different images came back to him: his uncle's face as he was sentenced, snatches of the prosecution's closing speech, noises and colors, remarks overheard. It all came to him in no apparent order, connected only by fear and anger. Still, Qaher realized it was unreasonable to worry about any sort of trial. Come on! He worked for a private company which had no legal powers. What could it do to him? At worst, fire him. And even that made no sense. But he couldn't help it; the desert was scoffing at him.

There it was, defying him, tormenting him, reminding him that power could draw on many more hidden resources than you would think. The words he'd heard when he first arrived here came back to him: a dead Bedouin doesn't matter.

Qaher was tempted to run. He was alone, sitting on the sand, under cover of darkness, with no one watching him; he hadn't committed any crime; the fire had nothing to do with him. He was free. Fadia was waiting for him. Fadia meant more to him than anything else. He didn't do it. Leaving in such unfavorable circumstances could have been interpreted as a confession of guilt. And he also realized that people here were at breaking point, ready to snap at anything or anyone without provocation.

When Qaher went back into the building, the engineer had managed to get hold of the investigators. They'd already been waiting a long time for him in the Company's administrative offices. He had to get back on the road. Qaher started up his car. It was nearly dawn.

43

The Kafkaesque situation started all over again in the Company's administrative offices. The investigators weren't there. They were about to arrive, the night watchmen told him, he'd just have to wait. Wait again. And yet he'd been told they'd be here. He must have misunderstood. The investigators had gone to Abu Dhabi in the middle of the night. He should wait. He should go up to the second floor. The investigators were on their way, they'd be here any minute.

A hard day was beginning to dawn. The direction in which the sealed windows faced meant he couldn't watch the sun come up over the horizon, but it was getting light. The sleepless night, the coffees, the waiting, and the irritation all contributed to a growing sense of unease. He felt dirty, on the outside and inside; his skin felt taut, as after a long flight. He wished he could take a shower. And this new day dawning worried him. He set off in search of a telephone, going from one floor to the next, until the investigators arrived.

They appeared in the bright, neon-lit foyer with the puffy faces of people who've just been woken. Hardly so much as a hello, only a wave of the hand for him to follow them, and they dived into the elevator. Once they reached their floor, they asked him to wait. To wait! He was surrounded by bland, unimaginative comforts. Gray carpeting, glass doors, air-conditioning. He waited.

When he was called into the room to answer some questions, he went in with total, exhausted detachment. What followed was an inept inquiry to which he responded without really concentrating. He was thinking about Fadia. From time to time he noticed, but didn't comment on, the investigators' incompetence on various technical points. He was also surprised to be asked a number of more personal, more insidious questions, but he dealt with these without paying much attention either. He was thinking about Fadia again. This performance went on until midday, when they were provided with meal trays. He asked several times to be allowed to make a telephone call, but was stopped on a variety of grounds.

The afternoon was given over to more questioning.

It was now seven o'clock and the interrogation had come to an end. He had to wait for a decision to be reached about him. Qaher thought the whole thing was laughable. The last few days he'd sometimes felt he'd turned into the person he used to be—mostly in spite of himself. But at the same time, the child he'd once been, with his thwarted hopes, constantly running into stupid, self-serving attitudes, had become a triumphant adult. He found the thought comforting.

He promised himself that, once this charade was over, he'd call Fadia and they could laugh about all this, as in the old days. As soon as it was over he'd find Fadia, and they'd go into the desert together. The desert in all its sobering freedom washes away absurdity far more efficiently than the sea ever can. Yes, they'd go into the desert. Tomorrow. This evening. He would talk to her. He suddenly knew what to say to her.

The door was flung open and Qaher woke from his daydream with a start. The two investigators were standing facing him but not actually looking at him. One of them handed him a letter. Qaher stood up and took the letter but didn't open it.

"Is it over?" he asked.

They nodded.

"Can I make a phone call now?"

They said he could.

Qaher slipped the letter into his pocket and ran into the corridor, into the elevator, into the entrance hall, all the way to reception, where he demanded a telephone. The secretary handed him a cordless phone and he grabbed it eagerly. He feverishly dialed the number he'd been repeating to himself for hours, and asked to speak to Fadia.

"Your friend's no longer here, sir," a woman told him. "She's left."

"What do you mean? Has she moved to different halls?"

"No. She's gone back to Syria."

"But why?"

"I don't know, sir, she didn't give me a reason."

44

The air-conditioning was always on too high at the Columbia Café. Today more than usual. It was cold. The last straw in this sun-drenched place. Qaher repressed a shiver. At the far end of the room a pianist—or rather a weary-looking shadow bent over a keyboard—unconvincingly plinked a few tired notes. The bar was deserted. In its nakedness, it was just a big gloomy room made somehow sinister by the absence of customers. The souks and beaches must be teeming with people at this time of day; in the oil and gas fields the massive machinery of metal and men must be droning as it toiled. Life was going on elsewhere.

Qaher heaved a sigh of resignation and shifted in his chair but failed to get comfortable. He hadn't succeeded since this morning, and had exhausted every possible position. His body was now aching. His four friends sat facing him, in shirt-sleeves, sipping drinks. Sector 8 hadn't started operating again yet, and they were passing the time. Nestled deep in the black leather chairs, they looked as if they'd been up all night drinking, exhausted, disheveled.

Qaher looked at them and thought about the desert. He thought about the letter the investigators had given him. He thought about Fadia, who'd left because he didn't turn up.

After all those months of faultless work, after being a scrupulous and attentive engineer, driving across the Habshan region in every direction, day and night . . . after all that, he'd been suspended. The Company had almost fired him, although it didn't actually accuse him of causing a fire for which he couldn't possibly be held responsible.

And yet the clinical way he was informed of his *temporary* suspension was nothing compared with the appalling news the switchboard operator had delivered when she said Fadia had left. Qaher had called the airport. In vain. And the office of Oman's minister for education. With no better result. Fadia had gone back to Syria, thinking God only knew what about him. He hadn't managed to talk to her or to stop her from leaving.

Laid off and with nothing to do, he'd ended up going to the scene of the disaster a few days later. To see, to touch with his own hands the incident that had so wronged him. The fire still wasn't completely under control, but the crisis was over. The sector's wells had been shut down, and all employees had left the site, leaving the firefighters in charge.

He'd stayed there a long time, gazing at the now inert derricks blackened by smoke. He'd tried to reconnect with the sense of power he'd felt when it was all working. But he failed. Something that had once seemed tangible, huge, and intense now felt dead in the forced inactivity before him. A massive lifeless skeleton disfiguring the landscape. All those thousands of men and machines he'd pictured working to the same rhythm, with the same purpose, delving into the ground—they'd all gone, disappeared, as if they'd never existed. That power was proving as pointless and false as the power he had butted up against as a child when he had to confront his grandmother's incomprehension and his father's contempt; it was as deceitful as the noise of the construction site had seemed once he'd witnessed his young uncle's sentencing. He left, feeling completely indifferent to this dead thing, indifferent to its fate.

"What are you thinking about, Qaher?" Durieux asked.

"Stop drinking. She'll come back, believe me," Alvaro muttered, pasty-mouthed.

"Leave him alone," Bensoussan intervened, even though it seemed to cost him a superhuman effort. Then, more or less mumbling to himself, he added, "We've drunk just as much as him."

"Come on, get a grip," Alvaro continued, ignoring the comment.

But Bensoussan kept going, his voice softening as he added thoughtfully, "Especially as nothing's changed, you know, it's only temporary."

Qaher looked up slowly. Apart from the time of day and recent events, this could have been one of those countless, tediously repetitive evenings he'd spent with them. Only yesterday he would have smiled at this; now he felt peculiarly moved.

"I was thinking about my childhood," he said. "The desert."

"The desert?"

"Yes . . . it's hard to tell my childhood and the desert apart."

"Do you mean it was empty?" Bensoussan asked. He was trying desperately to bring Qaher back to reality, back to his group of friends here and now. Despite his gloomy mood, Qaher couldn't help smiling.

"No, I mean I grew up in the desert."

Then he had an idea and suddenly sat up to have a good look at his four friends. Just then a low hum filled the room, a rhythmic, beating sound. The ceiling fans had been put on. The place would soon be filling up. Qaher looked at his friends, who'd now fallen silent one after the other, having tried to ease his pain in their own individual ways.

In light of the injustice visited on Qaher and of his own weakness, these people he'd always thought of as strangers were showing their more human side. Their drunken superficiality and their easy carefree life were giving way to a new compassion, to eye contact and gestures and words Qaher would never have expected from them. He was angry with himself for being so blind.

Cunning, he'd always tried to convince himself, helped overcome differences. But how wrong he'd been! He would never be anything but a Badawi, a child of the desert, and cunning would never eradicate that. Qaher had wanted to break away from his origins. He'd sat here with the others drinking stiff bourbons, he'd laughed and joked with them, he'd also silently despised them and sometimes envied them, but at the same time he'd become deaf to the beating of his own heart, he'd wanted to believe that he'd freed himself of the desert, and that it would never try to get him back again. The penalty inflicted on him by the Company was having an effect: it was opening his eyes. Just as Fadia had done.

David Bensoussan had forsaken his usual pessimism. It was only a temporary decision, he said again; they'd soon realize

Qaher had nothing to do with the accident. They'd end up apolo-
gizing and taking him back. Maybe David was right. Probably,
even. But that didn't matter.

Alvaro, who'd had more to drink than usual, had gone
into ecstasy over the old photo of Fadia that Qaher had been
keen to show them. He thought she was lovely, so much so
that Qaher was almost jealous. But his friend's slightly drink-
fueled words and his own mental picture of Fadia waiting for
him in vain had persuaded him not to comment. He had only
himself to blame.

Brint hadn't said anything specific. He'd come. That was
enough. The way he drank spoke for him. Strange as it may
seem, he was drinking because he shared Qaher's pain, and
the only way he knew to alleviate pain was to drink. What
did it matter then whether Brint understood what was really
hurting him? Just having him there, even if he didn't speak,
touched Qaher.

Durieux, on the other hand, had been angry and disgusted.
Qaher would never have suspected that of him. Unlike the others, Durieux hadn't tried to console him, hadn't told him to be
patient, hadn't pandered to his vanity, and hadn't shouldered his
pain. No. He'd told him to dump everything, abandon all this,
leave, start a new life. Qaher had listened—he wasn't far from
sharing this view—and in the end he realized that Durieux's
vehemence was nudging him toward doing what he himself
had never had the courage to do: to leave.

Qaher put down his half-empty glass. To think he'd always
said he didn't want to fail at anything! He got to his feet and
gestured to the others to stay sitting.

"I'm going out for a bit of a walk," he said.

But he'd taken only a couple of steps before he changed his mind; turned back toward his friends, who were still looking at him in surprised silence; and—not sure whether they'd actually understand—said:

"My name's Maïouf."

Then he headed for the doors and walked out of the Columbia Café.

45

There was no clear boundary at the top of the hills, as on that fateful day, that fateful night. Qaher listened intently. He could hear them, hear animals calling. Horses whinnying, goats bleating, foxes yelping. He couldn't see them, though. They felt so near and yet so far away, living beyond the miseries of mankind. It was all there, just as before: the desert, the sky, and the moon. A red moon, red as the oil fire that had lit up the sky. The expanse of sand stretched before him, curve after curve. No woman would lift the blanket and slip out of the tent. No dark shape would hurry through the darkness with a donkey. He was alone for all eternity. Alone in the middle of the desert.

Why had he come here? He'd answered a call. He'd driven from expressway to expressway, his mind a blank, until he reached this one which came to a sudden stop deep in the desert, an abrupt end as if the planners had run out of money to finish building it. A road suspended, in the middle of the desert. Was this one last joke? Or a sign? The stars overhead glimmered. He tried to see their reflection on the land. Pointless. There was no river here, and no woman would come to it. He took a step. Then another. He felt so clumsy, so unsure of himself! One more step.

His self-assurance grew as he walked into the darkness, as the last traces of humanity disappeared, as he left behind that absurdly truncated strip of asphalt, as he moved away from his car whose smell of fuel he could still make out, the same smell that used to hang over his father's truck which he so longed to ride in as a child. He headed deeper into the night, drawn by those dark shapes blocking the horizon, blacker than the night itself. He immediately recognized the slump and bulk of these dunes, and, in a perverse interplay of shadows, they reminded him of the churlish judge who sentenced his uncle, and they seemed to have been waiting all this time for him here, right here. Just a few ordinary dunes, accumulations of sand around his village.

He hurried on. He wanted to get away from this flat, stony ground. He wanted to press on into the dust, to hear the fine sand crunch beneath his feet. To trample that judge underfoot along with all those who judged his life. He was irresistibly drawn by the supple, shifting curves, the swelling waves which rose up into the sky, abolishing a sense of space, stretching into infinity. As in the old days. He wanted to get to that mysterious place where the land came to an end.

Before him was nothingness, empty space, darkness and shadow swallowing up life. Not a soul to chase away or to follow, but a fear to appease, as on that first day long ago. A hillside appeared. He climbed it. The plain spread out beneath Ishtar's twinkling gaze. Here and there a motionless glitter of light lent an eeriness to this forsaken place covered in unpromising mounds, this vast emptiness which had never been welcoming.

He sat down at the top of the rise to gather his thoughts. He stayed there a while, letting his eyes drink their fill of the darkness and the moon's soft light catching on stones. Then he had a sudden urge to see the river, an imperious need, for no apparent reason and with no sense of hope. But he didn't move. Not straightaway. He leaned forward, carefully untied his laces, took off his shoes and socks, and put them in a neat pile beside him.

Only then did he stand up. Barefoot, he set off down toward the plain which reminded him of days gone by, when he was a child, days full of promise for a better life, full of dreams and secret joys. With the first few steps he felt a sharp pain. It was such a long time since he'd trodden arid ground like this. His feet and legs and every part of him had lost the habit of the desert. As a child he'd walked barefoot so often. Fire and frost, the sharp stones, he'd known all that, experienced it, overcome it. He was rediscovering it now.

He was wearing European clothes. He hadn't planned or prepared anything; he'd simply answered a call. And even now he didn't know what he was aiming for or where he was heading. But he kept going, his feet bleeding, stifling his pain, hypnotized by the expansive sea of scorched earth swallowing the horizon. He knew perfectly well there wasn't a river. But still he went. He wanted to find the river as he remembered it, to see its banks, its shimmering salt flats.

Once, not all that long ago, he'd wanted to feel at one with the land, to blend into the darkness in order to forget his sorrows and fear and remorse. He hadn't succeeded. He was just a child at the time. Would he be man enough now? Suddenly, out of nowhere, he heard a lament, a sad funereal song sung by a thousand voices, from across the ages, for him and him alone, alone in the middle of the desert, a murmured keening, chanting, weeping full of heartbreak, all around him.

He doubled up as if he'd been struck, turned around, looked up at the sky, and peered into the shadows. The lament swirled around him, enveloping him. So he started to run, but it followed him. His feet were being ripped by the jagged stones, and the lament followed him. He blocked his ears, and the lament shut in around him, imprisoning him, more real to him than the sky and the earth. He wished he could cry, but found he couldn't, just as he hadn't been able to on that other night. He screamed to smother the chanting but it cut through his cries.

She went out like a fire
With no embers left to burn

The river, the tumultuous waters of the river would deliver him from it. The river over there, behind that dune, or that one, beyond the horizon, over there. His salvation. Maïouf launched himself into the darkness.

46

"Hello. Is that you? So, do you know where he is?"

"No idea. No one knows where he is."

"But I've had the letter! They know what caused the fire. It's nothing to do with him. His suspension's over."

"I know, David, I know! I've read the letter too."

"But where the hell's he gone and hidden himself?"

"If only I knew . . . He's just vanished."

47

Dear Fadia,

There was a story they told in my village about a woman who caught the eye of a prominent man. She didn't find him attractive but he was important, and she couldn't refuse his advances. In order to escape she offered him a deal. He would go to a hill and leave a bag containing two stones: one black and one white. She would then go to the hill, alone, and take one of the stones without looking in the bag. If she came back with the white stone she would be free. If she came back with the black one, she would be his. The man agreed to this.

But he put two black stones in the bag.

When she reached the hill, the woman opened the bag and looked inside. She saw the two black stones. She couldn't denounce the trick; that would have meant denouncing herself. So she took one of the stones and threw it as far as she could. When she returned she pretended to look everywhere for the stone she'd brought back. She couldn't find it so it was clear that she'd lost it.

"It doesn't matter," she said. "You need only check the color of the stone left in the bag, then you'll know what color the stone I took was . . ."

After what's happened, I'm worried you'll interpret that as a parable about the wiliness of women. That's not how I understand it. By telling you this story, I simply wanted to praise women's ability to get out of difficult situations without harming anyone. The Bedouin have learned that wisdom. I'm not a woman and I've forgotten that I was a Bedouin. But you . . . Well, I hope you'll be able to throw away the black stone of our relationship.

Ever since I left for France, we've lived with misunderstandings. But here I am sending you this last message to tell you how much meeting you turned my life upside down. Our reunions haven't given us enough time to relearn each other. I know I was in the wrong. I know you waited for me in Muscat. I could explain why I didn't come, why I couldn't warn you I wouldn't be there. I could, but it's too late. Fadia, you're the only woman I've loved, you're the woman whose absence devastates me—and that absence is now definitive through my own fault. But you were asking too much of me, or too soon. I mean that as a boyfriend, your only boyfriend. Your life is still yours for the taking. Even without me, particularly without me.

When I was with you I often felt you were looking through me. It wasn't me you saw, you saw someone better than me. Perhaps I came into your life too soon. You talked in terms of something absolute, of faithful commitments. We were still children when we made those commitments. The gravity of what we were taking on frightened me, it felt inhuman. I was wrong. I confess, I've sacrificed too much to tolerate failure, the very idea of failure. No man can cope with the inhuman. I wanted to tear down the dream. And I was wrong.

The desert that I once rejected has gotten under my skin now. I breathe its wild perfume. This huge expanse is empty of you and it's now empty of the possibility of you, of being loved by you; it's deprived of the child we could have had, the one you longed for, and expected to have; and this huge expanse is my fate suffocating me.

I so wish we could have brought back a bag filled with white stones. Forgive me, Fadia. I'm leaving with your image in my heart, with you by my side. I'm leaving and I'm releasing you from the oath that bound us. Be free, Fadia. And be happy. Be happy, Fadia, if you ever loved me.

48

Fadia put the letter down. Her throat was dry from talking, recounting her story. It had grown dark outside. She hadn't seen the night fall, stealing through the city's streets. Electric lights and oil lamps and the strong-smelling lamps in which mutton fat crackled—lamps that only had to be mentioned to bring back painful memories—were all mingling to light up Aleppo. The citadel was brightly lit this evening, as it was every evening, making it the pride of every local.

On that Friday, at that time of day, men would be coming home from prayer, and women waiting for them. But Fadia was alone, she was waiting for no one, and it was dark in the room where she sat.

She'd come home after work, but this day of the week was different. It was a day of prayer for everyone, and for her too. Except she had her own prayer, a prayer which asked nothing, a prayer with no praising or lamenting, a commemoration, without sadness or nostalgia. She'd sat down on finely woven cushions and started telling her story.

It was still daytime when she began, but it was a long story and now that night was falling, the room was steeped in shadows. Fadia didn't want to put on any lights, though. Feeling her way, she found the little glass of mint tea that she'd made and then forgotten, and she drank the now cold tea thirstily. She carefully put the glass with its gold ornamentation down on a copper tray.

The years hadn't hardened her but they hadn't brought her much joy either. She glanced briefly out of the window she'd left open. From where she was sitting she could see only the sky, a clear night sky. What did that poet say, the one Maïouf had introduced her to when he was still with her? That the pure ended up among the stars.

She gave a half smile, the smile he so loved when they were young. But had she smiled since those days? Then she scanned the sky. It was a game. She'd known for a long time, she'd found his star. Its shy, surreptitious glow shone among the others. You had to know it to find it. But once you'd found it, it was the only one you saw.

Fadia heaved a melancholy sigh. She had to perform this rite to the very end. The shadow she was talking to, the shadow listening to her, was waiting for the end. So she continued in a sad voice, emphasizing some of the words.

"There, my son, the son *I never had*, that's the story of the father *you should have had*."